PLAYING
with
Pleasure

NEW YORK TIMES BESTSELLING AUTHOR
ERIKA WILDE

PLEASURE HAS NEVER BEEN SO DECADENT . . .

Paige Moore has a fulfilling business designing couture corsets for her high profile clientele, but her love life is sorely lacking. Being burned in the worst way possible by Sawyer Burrows has left her guarded and wary when it comes to men and their motives. When her best friend presents her with an invitation to The Players Club, she embraces the chance to enjoy a hot night with a stranger, and finally put her past heartbreak, and Sawyer, behind her.

Sawyer knows he devastated Paige with his careless actions a year and a half ago, and he's lived every day since with those regrets. Now, seeing Paige at The Players Club, he knows this is his chance to make amends and prove that there is still something between them worth pursuing. If sensual pleasure is what Paige is looking for, then he intends to be the man to spend the night seducing every part of her.

Paige's surrender is Sawyer's ultimate goal, but once her desires are sated, will she give them the second chance they deserve?

Chapter One

THE BELL ON the door to Couture Corsets tinkled, announcing that a customer had just walked into Paige Moore's small boutique in Old Town San Diego, where she designed and sold custom-made corsets.

"It's just me," she heard her good friend Raina Beck call out.

Knowing Raina would just head to the back area of the shop where Paige did all her designing and creations, she continued hand sewing small seed pearls to an exquisite white satin corset she was making for a client's wedding night.

A moment later, Raina walked past the curtain of glittering crystals hanging in the doorway that separated the retail floor from the workroom. "Wow, that looks stunning," she said of the one-of-a-kind bridal corset, her voice laced with awe.

Paige glanced over her shoulder and grinned.

"Thanks. Once I add the crystal and lace embellishments along the bodice, this bride is going to knock her groom's pants off when he sees her in this corset."

Raina laughed. "Not a bad way to start off a marriage."

"What? By getting lucky?" Paige asked humorously as she set her needle and thread down on the nearby worktable that dominated the area.

"And being totally turned on by your new wife."

"Speaking of getting turned on," Paige said with a smirk as she eyed her cheerful friend. "You're glowing and smiling all the time, so things with Logan must be good, yes?"

"Really good," Raina admitted, her face flushing with happiness. "And I do have to say, it's nice having sex on a regular basis," she teased.

Paige sent her a mock glare. "Yeah, I wouldn't know, so stop bragging," she grumbled, even though she was genuinely thrilled that Raina had found a man who absolutely adored her. "What brings you by?"

"I have something for you," Raina said and handed her an envelope with the word *Welcome* embossed in black across the front.

Paige's eyes widened as she looked at the envelope. "Oh my God, is this an invitation to your wedding? I can't believe you didn't tell me…" Her words and excitement trailed off as she pulled out the card inside and read the message granting her a night at The Players Club, an exclusive, members-only sex club.

"Oh, wow," she breathed in surprise and glanced back at Raina. "I thought—"

"If I was getting married, you'd know about it before I sent out invitations because you'd be my maid of honor," Raina interrupted with a laugh. "Besides, I'm not even engaged yet. This invitation is for you," Raina went on with a grin. "The Players Club is a place where you can get down and dirty and freaky with a stranger, indulge in a fantasy, or try a particular kink that has piqued your interest."

"I have to say, that sounds very tempting."

Oh, yes, Paige was definitely intrigued. It had been a year and a half since she'd been with a man. A year and a half since the morning Sawyer Burrows had shattered her heart with his betrayal. And the thought of indulging in a night of hot sex with an anonymous guy was incredibly appealing. She needed to do *something* to finally shake Sawyer from her mind and thoughts and let the painful past go so she could move on with her life.

Easier said than done, but an evening at The Players Club was a good start to putting an end to her dry spell.

"There is one thing you need to know." Raina suddenly looked uncertain. "Logan told me that

Sawyer is a member of The Players Club. Which, in my opinion, could work to your advantage if he's there the night you decide to go."

Paige frowned, not sure how she felt about running into a man she swore she hated yet who still had the ability to affect her on a physical level. Yeah, that part drove her absolutely crazy, but she was curious what Raina meant. "How so?"

"*If* he's there, think of it as a bit of revenge." Raina's eyes danced with mischief. "Flirt with other guys and enjoy yourself. Show Sawyer exactly what he's been missing and what is no longer his. Men are such jealous, possessive creatures, and it'll drive him nuts to see you with another man."

The corner of Paige's mouth curled into a smile as she thought about her friend's suggestion. It had been too long since she'd felt desired and sexy. Combine the bonus of possibly showing Sawyer that she was over him by letting him see her enjoy another man's attention, and it really was a win-win situation.

Her decision made, she met Raina's gaze and lifted her chin in determination. "I'm totally down for that."

Chapter Two

One week later…

THE LOUNGE AREA to The Players Club was incredibly lush and elegant but much more relaxed than Paige had anticipated, which helped to calm the butterflies fluttering in her belly. The glass of wine she'd ordered from the bartender—per the club's two-drink-max rule—also helped to soothe the nervous energy coursing through her.

She'd never been to a sex club before, and from the moment she'd walked into the huge mansion, she'd known she was definitely out of her element. Especially since she was probably the only one there who'd yet to pop her sex club cherry, she thought in amusement. But so far, everyone had been friendly and welcoming, and she had to admit that she felt very comfortable and no pressure from the few men who'd already approached her with definite interest in their eyes. Which was also a nice little boost to her confidence.

Then again, it didn't hurt that she was wearing a custom-fitted corset that cinched in her waist, plumped up her full breasts, and gave her Kardashian curves. She'd paired the purple-and-black-embroidered corset with a black leather miniskirt and four-inch heels that Raina had assured her did amazing things for her legs. Paige had always been a little on the plus-size, and it was hard not to compare herself to the other gorgeous, slender women in the room with the kind of centerfold figures that most men preferred.

Sawyer included.

She groaned to herself as the unwanted thought popped into her head, but that painful truth was difficult for her to forget, considering Sawyer had slept with Paige's Barbie look-alike stepsister, Ashley, *while* he'd been dating Paige. The memory still had the ability to make her feel as though someone had punched her in the stomach, as did her stepsister's words after Paige had caught them together.

Paige, you can't expect a hot, gorgeous guy like Sawyer to be content and satisfied with someone as big and fat as you. Men like him want a woman who is slender and beautiful, who doesn't have a belly and chubby thighs. He told me he just felt sorry for you...

That flashback was enough to bring all of her insecurities bubbling to the surface and make her question what the heck she was doing in a place like The Players Club. She certainly couldn't compete with the other attractive, seductive women in the lounge, and in a moment of panic, she abruptly turned around to leave—and bumped full force into a solid male chest that stopped her short, nearly sloshing her wine onto the both of them. A pair of strong hands caught her by the arms to steady her.

"Oh my God," she gasped, her cheeks flushing in embarrassment as she looked up into a handsome face. "I'm so sorry. I should have looked where I was going."

"No worries." He smiled and slowly released his hold on her, his head tipping to the side in undeniable interest. "I enjoyed running into you," he teased. "My name is Dane."

He seemed friendly, and knowing it would be rude to continue her mad dash to the exit without a reply, she exhaled a deep breath and returned his smile. "It's nice to meet you. I'm Paige."

He pushed his hands into the front pockets of his slacks, obviously in no hurry to move on as he studied her face. "You're new here, aren't you?"

The flush on her cheeks escalated to a slow heat, that he'd so easily pegged her for a newbie. "Is it that obvious?"

He laughed, the sound warm and engaging. "Actually, I have a thing for redheads," he said and lifted a hand to follow the end of a soft, wavy strand that curled against the upper swell of her breast. "You caught my eye the moment you walked into the lounge. If you'd been here before, I would have remembered you."

The desire in his eyes as he glanced from her cleavage to her mouth and back to her gaze should have elicited some kind of physical reaction from her but, unfortunately, didn't. "I'm a first timer," she admitted.

He dropped his hand back down to his side, displaying all signs of a true gentleman, which she appreciated. "Then I insist on giving you a personal tour of the place," he said amicably. "Just as soon as I get myself a drink. Would you like a refill on your wine?"

She shook her head, wanting to be sure she kept a clear head. "No, I'm fine. Thank you."

"Then I'll be right back."

Paige watched him walk toward the bar. Unfortunately, she felt no spark between them, and she sighed. She really wished otherwise, because not only was the man good-looking but he was a genuinely nice guy. But she'd told herself before arriving that if she was going to be with anyone tonight, there had to be some kind of chemistry and a mutual attraction. Straight-out lust would even be better. Regardless, she planned to leave the club afterward without any kind of personal attachments to complicate matters.

Maybe, while she and Dane were perusing the club, things would change, and she'd find him more sexually attractive, she thought as she took another sip of her wine.

While she waited for him to return, she glanced around the lounge. New men and women had arrived and were talking and mingling, while others had paired up and were sitting together in one of the intimate, den-like areas across the room, which Paige had just noticed. Her curious gaze swept along each of the secluded spots and the couples within, some of which had opted to release the sheer drapes tied off on either side of the alcove for more privacy.

And that's when she saw him—*Sawyer*—casually sitting on one of those velvet couches while a gorgeous and perfectly built woman was draped across his lap with her arms around his neck. One of his hands was on her hip, the other rested on her thigh, and the long-haired brunette was smiling at Sawyer in a way that was familiar and seductive as she leaned in close and said something in his ear.

Shock riveted Paige's feet to the floor as she watched his full lips move as he issued some kind of response. Paige's mind screamed at her to *look away* before he caught her, but instead, her traitorous gaze lifted from his mouth to his eyes. She sucked in a sharp breath as her gaze collided with his, and even from across the room, she could feel his intense, heated stare, focused on *her* like a laser.

An unexpected—and definitely unwanted—surge of desire poured through her, and a traitorous ache settled between her thighs. She desperately tried to ignore both, reminding herself despite the fact that Sawyer still had the ability to make her body come alive with just a look, there was no forgiving him for what he'd done to her. Pretending as though seeing him there at the club had absolutely no effect on her at all was one of the most difficult things she'd ever had to do, but she forced herself to remain indifferent and glanced away just as Dane arrived back by her side with his drink in hand.

"Ready for your tour?" he asked and offered her his arm in a charming fashion.

Grateful for something to hold on to so her weak knees wouldn't buckle, she slipped her hand through the crook of his arm and gave Dane a smile. "I'm looking forward to it."

For the next half hour, he escorted her through the mansion, which kept her mind distracted with all the various activities the club had to offer—themed fantasy boudoirs, viewing rooms, open playrooms, and the dark and intense dungeon. In the lower level, a Mardi Gras-themed party was in full swing, complete with beads being awarded for naked breasts while other couples openly kissed and groped and fucked.

They ended up back at the lobby area, standing in front of the split staircase that led to two separate wings of the house where the public and private rooms were located. Another stairway led down to the dungeon with all its Medieval-like furniture and contraptions that were way out of her first-timer league.

Dane turned to face her, his gaze clearly expressing his interest in her. "I'm heading down to the dungeon, which is my personal preference here at the club," he said, holding her hand in his. "Care to join me?"

"I don't think I'm ready for all that." Paige wouldn't have pegged him for a man who enjoyed those mock torture devices, but hey, she wasn't one to judge. And considering there was still no chemistry or any kind of sexual tension on her end, she decided it was time to part ways.

"I'm going to walk through the viewing rooms upstairs and get a better feel for what interests me," she told him.

"Good girl," he said, clearly respecting her decision, despite the flicker of disappointment in his gaze.

"Never do anything that makes you feel uncomfortable or that's out of your comfort zone. That said, if you change your mind and want to play in the dungeon, I'd enjoy being your partner for the night."

She didn't see that happening. "It was nice meeting you, Dane."

He strolled downstairs, and Paige climbed the winding staircase to the second level, wondering if she was going to be able to find a man tonight worth ending her year-and-a-half sexual drought.

WHAT THE FUCK was *she* doing here?

It was the first thought that leapt into Sawyer's mind the moment he caught sight of Paige in The Players Club lounge. There was no mistaking the rich shade of her wavy auburn hair he used to love wrapping around his hands or the voluptuous curves of her body she tried to conceal beneath the corset she wore. Both had been embedded in his brain for the past year and a half, slipping into his dreams at night and taunting him with the way her soft skin felt beneath his hands and how sweet her breasts tasted in his mouth.

Shock didn't even come close to describing the emotion that tightened his chest or the way every muscle in his body tensed when her vivid green eyes met and held his from across the room.

He'd seen her briefly a few weeks ago at Raina Beck's shop—their very first encounter since he'd left for his fifteen-month, and final, tour in Iraq. It had also been the first time he'd seen Paige since that awful morning after waking up in her stepsister's bed, naked, disoriented, and his head pounding like a motherfucker.

Yeah, that was another less pleasant memory firmly seated in his brain, as was the absolute horror of realizing that he'd slept with Ashley—the evidence of fucking her indisputable. There was no forgetting how she'd cuddled up to him, her hand on his dick to try and persuade him into a morning quickie, but he hadn't been able to get out of her bed fast enough. She'd pouted unhappily, like the spoiled rich girl she was, while he'd pulled on his pants, shoved his feet into his shoes, and grabbed his shirt before racing out of her room and down the grand spiral staircase in the opulent mansion where Paige lived with her stepsister and stepmother.

He had no fucking idea how he'd ended up in Ashley's room. His only thought at the time was that he'd had too much to drink the night before at Paige's birthday party and had done the unthinkable—and how the fuck was he going to explain this to Paige? Just as he'd reached the entryway, his stomach roiling,

Paige had walked out of the adjoining living room. She'd frozen in place when she'd seen him, her gaze traveling from his disheveled, half-naked state to her stepsister, Ashley, who had chased after him in nothing but a robe that was sheer enough to see that she had nothing on beneath.

He'd been caught in the act, and the devastation that had played across Paige's features in that moment had destroyed him, as well. He'd crossed the marbled foyer to talk to her, very aware of Ashley watching the whole scenario play out from where she was standing at the top of the stairs.

He'd stopped in front of Paige, the bright pain in her eyes equivalent to a knife twisting in his heart. He wanted so badly to touch her, to reassure her, but how could he explain something that he didn't even understand himself?

"Paige ..." His voice had been like gravel, and he'd whispered the only thing he could. "I'm so sorry."

She'd slapped him hard across the cheek, trying so valiantly to keep the tears shimmering in her eyes in check. "You're a fucking asshole." Lifting her chin in an attempt to salvage her pride, she'd turned around and walked away.

Utterly defeated and racked with guilt, he'd headed back toward the front door, not sure how he was going to repair the damage he'd done. When he'd glanced up at Ashley, the smug smile on her face had made his gut churn. The goddamn bitch was actually *pleased* that she'd just shattered her sister's happiness, and he'd had the sickening feeling that he'd fallen into some kind of trap of Ashley's making.

Even after leaving the house that morning, he'd tried to text and call Paige, until she'd blocked his phone number, making it very clear that they were over. And because he had no excuse for what he'd done, he'd respected her decision. Five days after that, he'd been deployed to Iraq, and he'd spent the next fifteen months immersed in guilt as he replayed that morning over and over in his mind.

He'd probably never know the real truth of how he'd ended up in Ashley's bed, but he definitely had his suspicions.

"You seem distracted tonight," the woman sitting on his lap said into Sawyer's ear, bringing his thoughts back to the present. "What's going on with you?"

Jenny was someone he occasionally hooked up with at The Players Club. Neither of them was looking for a commitment, so their arrangement worked well. She liked being tied up and restrained and enjoyed a bit of pain with her pleasure, which matched perfectly with Sawyer's own need to dominate and be in control. That was a part of himself he'd hidden from Paige when they'd dated, because he'd wanted to be sure they had a solid relationship, as well as trust between them, before he introduced her to his penchant for ropes and showed her how a twinge of pain could heighten her own desires.

It had taken him weeks to coax Paige into being confident about her body and sensuality, to make her believe that she was sexy and desirable exactly the way she was. In fact, that night on her birthday, he'd planned to show her just how good it felt to let him be completely in control of her pleasure…only to have her sister obliterate everything between them.

Still ensnared by Paige's gaze, he absently replied to Jenny's question without looking away. "I've just got a lot on my mind."

She trailed her fingers from around his neck and down the front of his shirt. "Maybe I can give you something else to think about," she murmured huskily, her insinuation clear.

Paige was the first to break eye contact with him, appearing completely unaffected by his presence, which only served to irritate the shit out of him since his insides were tangled up in a knot when he thought about the reasons *she* was here at the club. Dane, a regular at the mansion who enjoyed his encounters with women more on the hard-core side of things, walked up to Paige, offered his arm, and escorted her out of the lounge.

Jealousy shot through Sawyer like a hot spear, along with something darker and more possessive he couldn't subdue, no matter how hard he tried. He still wanted Paige, in every way imaginable, and the thought of another man touching her brought out the beast in him, as well as triggered the need to be the one to master her body and mind.

And that's when he decided that if any man was going to introduce Paige to any sort of forbidden limits, it was going to be *him*.

Jenny nuzzled her lips against his neck, reminding Sawyer that he still had a very willing female sitting on his lap. One he suddenly had no interest in at all.

He tipped her face up to his and gently said, "I'm really sorry, Jenny, but there's something personal I have to take care of tonight."

Her smile was tinged with disappointment, but he knew she understood. They weren't exclusive in any way, and there were plenty of other men in the room who'd enjoy what Jenny had to offer.

She slid off his lap and looked into his eyes. "I hope she's worth it," she said softly.

Paige was. Always had been, and always would be.

Chapter Three

PAIGE STOOD AGAINST the decorative wrought
iron railing that wrapped around the second-floor
balcony of the club and overlooked the public playrooms below. The unobstructed view from above was
enlightening, highly arousing, and she was riveted by
all the various scenarios and debauchery playing out
for anyone to see.

She'd chosen a private and darkened corner so she
could observe the erotic settings and scenes freely and
openly and without feeling awkward or uncomfortable
around other members. There were women restrained
to spanking benches who clearly enjoyed being pad-
dled by their partner. In another section, a woman was
harnessed to a sex swing while the man she was with,
who was dressed in leather and wore a black hood to
disguise his face, used a steel wand that emitted
electrical pulses whenever he touched the object to the

her bare breasts or the sensitive skin along her inner thigh.

Paige winced at the thought of being Tasered, even though the woman's cries of passion begged her partner for more—and he was more than happy to oblige. That kind of elevated torture was so not her thing, and her gaze quickly moved on from that scene to another sectioned-off area that was designed like a jail cell with a small bed.

Two men dressed in police uniforms had a woman standing with her hands against the wall as they stripped off her clothing and roughly frisked her, their hands searching everywhere. When fingers probed between her legs, she put up a token struggle, which earned her a sharp slap to her ass from one of the cops while the other handcuffed her wrists behind her back for her insubordination.

Paige couldn't look away and didn't want to, judging by the rush of heat flowing through her veins and the tight pucker of her nipples. The trio obviously wanted an audience since they were in the public domain, and from her secluded spot on the upper floor, there was no reason why she couldn't enjoy the titillating show. Even if this was all she ended up doing this evening, the heady cop fantasy unfolding in front of her was one she could replay in her mind night after night.

One of the officers stripped off his shirt and sat down on the cot. He unzipped his uniform pants, released his stiff cock, and stroked the length while officer number two pushed their female lawbreaker onto her knees in front of the first dark-haired cop. He grabbed a fistful of her hair and pulled her closer, and with her hands still restrained at the base of her spine, she had no choice but to comply. He thrust his dick between her parted lips, and the man behind her secured a strong arm around her waist to lift up her hips, then he lowered his head and put his mouth between her legs.

Oh God. Paige wrapped her hands around the railing in front of her. Her breathing deepened, her sex pulsed, and she pressed her thighs together to alleviate the growing ache building steadily in between. She was so damn tempted to touch herself, to give her body the release it was suddenly screaming for.

"You like to watch."

The deep, male voice directly behind Paige made her jump. The fact that the sexy-as-sin timbre belonged to Sawyer made her insides quiver and amped up the lust that was making her more and more restless by the minute. He wasn't touching her, but she could feel the heat of his body, could smell the familiar spice of man and cologne. Every part of her responded to his scent—breasts swelling and pussy clenching—and she hated that he still had the ability to make her crave his touch.

She didn't turn around. Instead, she shored up her defenses, refusing to allow him to see or hear how vulnerable he made her feel. "Watching is safe," she said, proud of how strong her voice sounded.

"But not nearly as satisfying," he murmured, his seductive words a tease that added another layer of desire to build inside of her.

He placed his hands on her waist, and she swallowed back a gasp, shocked by the bold move. She was grateful for the barrier of her corset stays and the heavy fabric that protected her from skin-to-skin contact with this man. She didn't think she could handle the actual *feel* of his hands on her.

She tightened her fingers around the railing and tried to sound blasé, when she was anything but indifferent to him. "What do you want, Sawyer?"

"You."

Just like that, the past crashed through her…how he'd always made her feel so desired and beautiful and how he'd ultimately betrayed her with Ashley.

Her emotions suddenly felt chafed raw, and she swallowed back the lump that formed in her throat. "I want to hate you," she said, truly wishing she could. Lord knew she'd tried to despise him for the way he'd hurt her, but there was no denying that her heart wanted to forgive him. It was a constant tug-of-war she struggled with.

"You *should* hate me," he said, moving closer so that the front of his body aligned with the back of hers in one long, lean wall of muscle and heat. His low, husky voice, tinged with regrets, whispered in her ear, "But not tonight."

She wasn't sure what to make of that statement, but her body wanted to believe that tonight, the need smoldering within her was mutual.

"What are you doing here, Paige?" he asked huski-ly.

A few minutes ago, she would have replied with a callous *I'm here to get laid* just to irk him, but instead, she answered more honestly. "I'm here for pleasure."

Still behind her, he slid his hands over the swell of her hips and down the sides of her leather miniskirt until he reached the hem. "Then let me be the one to give it to you."

Again, her response should have been a succinct *screw you*, followed up with her elbow ramming into his ribs to make him move away, but she couldn't say or do either. But the words that *did* come out of her mouth were just as brash. "What about your date? Don't you think she'll be pissed off when she finds out you're with another woman? Oh, wait, I forgot, that's how you roll."

She heard him swear beneath his breath at her dig, but surprisingly, he didn't take his hands off her like she expected. Instead, he gripped the hem of her skirt in his fists and gradually inched it up. "I didn't come here with a woman," he said in a soft growl. "Right here, right now, *you're* the only woman I want. If you don't want this, say the club's safe word now, because once I touch you, *really* touch you, I'm not stopping until I make you come."

Stunned by the promise in his voice, in his words, she could barely breathe, let alone speak. And did she really want to? she thought, aching for what he was offering. With him standing behind her and out of her sight, she could pretend he was that sexy stranger she'd intended to hook up with tonight. He could be anything and anyone she wanted him to be.

Her heart raced as he dragged her skirt up higher and higher, until the material was bunched around her hips and the cool air kissed the exposed skin where the tops of her lacy thigh-high stockings ended. He wedged a knee between her legs, forcing her high heels apart, and she bit back a moan when his fingers traced the elastic band of her panties all the way down to her covered mound.

"Watch the scene below," Sawyer ordered, using a commanding tone she'd never heard from him before.

That authoritative voice excited her. Thrilled her.

And made her wetter than she already was.

She shifted her gaze back to the two cops and the woman in the makeshift jail cell—one man fucking her mouth and the other now pumping hard and deep into her from behind. Having two men at once wasn't a reality Paige ever wanted for herself, but the fantasy was incredibly hot to witness. As was the level of authority and dominance the two imposing officers exerted over their restrained prisoner, forcing the woman to submit to their ruthless possession.

Sawyer pulled the crotch of her panties to one side and dipped the fingers of his other hand along her slick pussy, a low, agonized groan escaping him. "Jesus, Paige. You're so fucking hot and soft and *drenched*."

She shivered at his dirty, unrefined description, and a warm flush swept across her cheeks. He stroked back and forth, spreading her moisture along her slit, then burrowed two long fingers into the folds on either side of her swollen clit. He gently tugged and plucked that bundle of nerves between his fingers, sending a shockwave of pleasure pulsing deep within her sex.

She bit her bottom lip, clutching the wrought iron just in case her trembling legs buckled on her as he continued the stimulating friction, the exhilarating and erotic pull on her clit—each time a little harder, a little sharper, inflicting just enough of a sting to keep her on the sweet edge of release.

Beyond wild for that orgasm he held just beyond her reach, she closed her eyes and dropped her head back onto Sawyer's shoulder, no longer caring about the scene below when she was so close to her own orgasm. One more wicked flick of his fingers across her clit jolted her with another electric shock of ecstasy, dragging a moan from her throat as the initial tingle of pain dissolved into a liquid heat that spread throughout her sex.

Sawyer had never, ever touched her in such an insistent, relentless way that *demanded* her surrender. And dear Lord, she was helpless to resist him and the promise of something so powerful and explosive. With shameless abandon, she pushed her hips back against his. His erection, huge and rock hard, so deliciously hot and thick, pressed along the crease of her ass while his fingers did insanely sinful things to her pussy.

His own breathing was hot and damp and harsh against her cheek, and he secured his other arm around her waist, as if knowing she'd need the anchor once she splintered apart. His entire body wrapped around her—protectively and possessively—and the glide and friction of his fingers between her legs commanded her acquiescence, allowing her no escape and no retreat from the pleasure about to consume her.

"Give it to me," Sawyer rasped into her ear. "*Now.*"

As if he'd given her permission to come, desire bloomed fast and fierce. The beginning spasms of a massive orgasm started deep inside of her and radiated outward, giving her no choice but to embrace the overwhelming sensations assailing her mind and body. She released a soft cry and tried to catch her breath once the tremors subsided.

Slowly, he removed his fingers and pulled the hem of her skirt back in place. "Fuck, that was hot," he breathed against the side of her neck.

"I can't believe I let you do that to me out in the open." Embarrassed by her actions, even though they were in a secluded alcove, she tried to move away from him, but he planted his strong hands back on her waist to hold her in place.

"Apparently, not only are you a voyeur but you have a bit of an exhibitionist streak in you, as well." Amusement softened the rough edges of sexual tension still lingering in his voice.

No, not really. She didn't have the kind of body she'd ever feel comfortable flaunting naked.

"Tell me, Paige," he murmured, his voice suddenly dark and daring. "Do you want more pleasure?"

She hated how his question made her tremble and

caused her to flush with renewed excitement—like a drug addict being offered another hit of their favorite opiate. In her case, it was sex. She knew she ought to be smart and say no and walk away, but this new and dominant edge to Sawyer definitely intrigued her. And as long as she compartmentalized the physical from the emotional and set some ground rules to protect her heart, why couldn't she enjoy a night of pleasure— not with a stranger but a man she trusted with her body? In that regard, at least, he'd never hurt her, and he was the safer decision.

She exhaled a deep breath and replied before she changed her mind. "Yes, I want more pleasure."

He stepped back, and for a moment, she thought *he'd* changed his mind. She turned around to face him, and with him standing only a foot away, she was struck with just how gorgeous he truly was. *Way-out-of-your-league kind of gorgeous*, as her stepsister had once told her, and a part of her couldn't help but think that, too.

His black hair was still cut military short at the sides, and with his masculine features and strong jawline, he could have easily made a fortune as a male model. Even with the dark, evening stubble on his face, the man was breathtaking—and she knew the body beneath the black shirt and pants was equally honed and impressive.

"Come with me," he said and held out his hand to

her.

His gaze was filled with a hypnotic blend of heat and promise. The hand he offered was a request for her trust, and she refused to analyze her actions as she touched her fingers to his warm palm, giving him the consent he was waiting for. She didn't miss the relief that passed across his features before he led her out of the viewing room and toward the private suites located in the opposite wing of the mansion. He bypassed all the normal playrooms and stopped in front of a closed door painted a rich shade of purple. The word VA-CANT on the digital keypad on the wall let them know the room was empty.

She hadn't seen this part of the mansion when Dane had given her a tour earlier. "Where are we?" she asked.

He inserted a code, and as the door unlocked, Sawyer glanced at her. "The suites back here are part of an exclusive membership. And by inputting my password, it lets the attendants know that the room is now occupied, and by whom."

Safety first. Okay, he'd obviously done this before, probably with the attractive brunette he'd been with in the lounge. She pushed that thought right out of her head. Tonight, she was more curious to find out what was behind the purple door and why it required an exclusive membership.

He opened the door for her, and she stepped inside. The room was small but more luxuriously and elegantly furnished than the others she'd seen. A four-poster dais dominated the space and was covered in fresh, deep purple linens the color of amethysts. Mirrors lined the walls throughout and were inlaid in the canopy and headboard of the poster bed, and most of the apparatuses (i.e., sex furniture) were covered in leather or velvet.

Undeniably fascinated, she stepped farther inside and continued to take it all in. There were hooks, chains, and restraints hanging from the ceiling, and shelves of implements and objects she couldn't recognize in the dim lighting. A wooden and brass rack held an assortment of floggers, canes, and crops, and when she inhaled, she breathed in the pleasant scent of lemon oil polish.

The door closing and locking behind her made Paige turn around. Sawyer stood there, silently watching her, obviously trying to gauge her reaction to this darker, more dominant part of him she'd had no clue existed. What else didn't she know about Sawyer and his predilections?

She smiled a bit nervously. "I had no idea you had a penchant for whips and chains and all...*this*," she said, waving her hand to encompass the room and all its BDSM devices.

He moved toward her, slowly and cautiously. "Sweetheart, I've *always* had these tendencies," he drawled, the revelation surprising her. "I just didn't want to scare you away."

He stopped in front of her, and she swallowed hard, trying to wrap her mind around the fact that he'd embraced vanilla sex with her while they'd been dating—*amazing* vanilla sex with hot fudge, whipped cream, and a cherry on top—because he'd been more worried about her reaction to his other sexual vices.

"And now?" she asked, wondering if he still had those concerns.

He lifted a hand and rubbed his thumb along her bottom lip, the caress sensual and erotic at the same time. "Are you scared?" he asked.

It sounded like a dare, and she answered with the truth. "No." If anything, she was fascinated and, deep down inside, excited.

"Then that's all that matters right now." He strolled to a dresser drawer and pulled out what looked like a coil of red rope. A wicked light flickered in his gaze as he returned to her. "Are you ready to step into my world of pleasure for a while?"

The moment of truth had her heart fluttering, but there was no denying the desire gathering force inside her. "Yes."

"Give me your hands, wrist to wrist," he instructed, and when she lifted them, he began wrapping and looping and knotting the silken cord with expertise. Once he had her hands bound, he checked to make sure he could fit two fingers between the rope and her skin to maintain her circulation. "Your safe word applies here. If, at any time, you're uncomfortable and you want me to stop what I'm doing, just say *red*."

She suddenly felt extremely vulnerable, and a moment of panic surged through her. "Red," she blurted out, not wanting to go any further until he assured her of a few things.

The fingers skimming across her wrists immediately stopped, and he raised his gaze to hers in surprise. "You want to end this?" he asked, his deep voice giving nothing away.

She shook her head, realizing just how serious he was about her mental and physical well-being, which she appreciated. "I didn't mean *stop*, stop," she rushed to say. "I just wanted you to wait a minute so I could lay down my hard limits."

He let go of her restrained hands and crossed his arms over his chest. "Okay. I'm all about respecting limits."

God, he looked so in his element in here, and she was undeniably attracted to all that power and control emanating off him. She wanted this, wanted *him*, but she wasn't going into this encounter without shoring up her defenses the only way she knew how. "I want to wear a blindfold, and you can take everything off me but my corset. And no kissing on the lips."

A flicker of emotion crossed his features, gone too fast for her figure out what it meant. It was quickly replaced by the quirk of his mouth as he oh-so-casually pulled the hem of his shirt from his pants.

"Okay," he agreed easily enough, though the slight narrowing of his gaze made her shift anxiously on her heels. "So, just to reiterate and make sure I have all this straight, you want a blindfold because then you can pretend I'm anyone you want me to be and make this a fantasy, instead of reality." He began unbuttoning his shirt, distracting her with the slow reveal of his muscular chest all the way down to tight, washboard abs. "You want your corset left on because it makes for a good, solid physical barrier between us." He shrugged out of the shirt and tossed it onto a nearby chair, then reached out and trailed a lazy finger along the lace-edged top of her bustier, making her nipples peak hard against the brocade fabric. "And no kissing on the lips because that's just *way* too intimate."

Her face flamed with embarrassment that she was so transparent, but she refused to back down. "Those are my rules. Take them or leave them."

"Oh, I'll definitely take them, sweetheart," he said with a bad-boy grin that shot heat straight to her core.

Chapter Four

PAIGE WATCHED SAWYER walk away again. He opened another drawer and retrieved a black silk mask, allowing her to look her fill of his backside before he concealed her vision. His shoulders were broad, the slope of his spine toned, and he had such a great, firm ass. When he turned around, her gaze was level with the front of his pants and what was hidden behind that impressive bulge in his fly as he strolled back toward her.

She dragged her gaze higher, her mouth watering as she followed the dark line of hair above the waistband of his pants to his belly button and all the way up to the light stubble on his face and the hot, carnal look in his dark brown eyes. Every single thing about Sawyer was so virile and heart-stoppingly male, and a part of her almost regretted having her hands bound because she would have loved touching all of him.

Everywhere.

He slipped the blindfold over her eyes, adjusting the silky fabric so that everything was pitch black. He grasped the knotted rope between her wrists and gave it a light tug, signaling her to follow his lead. Belatedly, she questioned the wisdom of demanding a mask, because she realized just how much trust it required on her end not to be able to see or anticipate what he planned to do to her. But she felt no fear, just a quickening desire and breathless excitement.

He brought her to a stop, then lifted her arms above her head and clipped something around the cord securing her hands so that her body was stretched taut. Any higher and she would have had to balance on the tips of her shoes.

"Are you comfortable?" he asked, his voice drifting in her ear from behind her. "Wrists feel okay?"

Other than feeling a little nervous and exposed, even though she was still completely dressed, she was fine. "I'm good."

She heard him move around her again, sensed him in front of her before his voice confirmed his position inches away. "Then let's get rid of this skirt, since it wasn't on your do-not-remove list."

The humor in his voice relaxed her, but the moment his fingers traced the waistband of her skirt around to her back, her skin tingled with awareness—

awareness of the fact that the front of his body was now pressed intimately against hers as he unfastened the button, then of the subtle brush of his warm lips along the side of her throat as he slowly lowered the zipper over the curve of her ass.

Her breathing hitched and she tensed. Sawyer hadn't violated any of her rules, but she suddenly realized it didn't matter how she'd tried to protect herself. This man was a master at seduction and adept at making her burn. Despite any restrictions she'd tried to implement, he'd find a way to unravel every one of her defenses and lay her desires bare.

And the only thing that would stop him was her using the safe word.

He didn't push her skirt off—yet. Instead, his hands came up and threaded into her hair, tugging gently on the strands. He tipped her head to the side and kissed his way along her neck until he reached her ear.

"Sweetheart," he said in a soft, cajoling tone that calmed her skittish thoughts. "I need you to get out of your head and let go. Give yourself and your pleasure over to me. Don't think. Just *feel*. I swear, it'll feel so fucking good if you do."

She shivered and moaned, believing him. Trusting him. She exhaled a deep breath, and along with it, she released all the tension in her body. Determined to *enjoy this*, she relaxed, allowing her limbs to go slack.

"Good girl," he praised and skimmed his hands back down to her skirt. His fingers slid into the waistband and slowly pushed the material down her hips and over her bottom, until it loosened and fell to the floor around her feet.

He shifted away, and the next thing she knew, he was kneeling in front of her, his fingers wrapping around one ankle to lift her foot, then the other, so he could get her skirt out of the way. He braced her feet wide apart, then smoothed his hands up her legs, his palms creating a delicious heated friction against the silk stockings she wore until he reached the lacy edges.

Her stomach tumbled when she felt the soft brush of his lips along the sensitive patch of skin of her inner thigh, and she moaned as his hot, wet tongue leisurely licked a path upward. He nuzzled her through her panties and nipped at her swollen flesh through the thin silk fabric, making her shiver with renewed hunger.

She might have made kissing her lips off limits, but he clearly had no qualms about putting that mouth everywhere else.

"The way you smell, especially after you come, always makes me so damn hard," he said, a dark, forbidden kind of lust infusing his deep voice. "I'm dying to taste you but not yet."

The fact that he remembered something so intimate surprised Paige, and her entire body went liquid at the wicked images that flitted through her mind of him burying his mouth between her thighs and exploring every inch of her pussy with his lips and tongue.

"First, you need to be punished," he said, instantly dissolving those sinful thoughts as she felt him stand back up. "So, what'll be, Paige? A paddle or a crop?"

Shock rippled through her. He'd never used any kind of discipline-type toys on her before, but hadn't he just warned her that he'd always had these kinds of sexual preferences, that he enjoyed adding a bit of pain to the pleasure? And what did he need to chastise her for? she wondered in confusion.

"Tell me now, or I'll choose for you." His tone was a sharp, demanding order.

"The crop," she said quickly, selecting what she thought would be the lesser of two evils. She'd seen and touched both in Raina's shop, had even been curious how they'd feel on her flesh, and decided the sting of a crop's leather tip would smart less than a wide wooden paddle.

When she heard him retrieve something from the nearby rack, a rush of adrenaline amped up the anticipation of the unknown. "Why do I need to be punished?"

The footsteps on the wooden floor came to a stop

beside her. "This is for you taking away the opportunity to look into your eyes when I slide deep inside of you," he said and snapped the leather crop in quick succession against the back of both of her thighs, right at the curve of her ass.

It felt as though she'd been stung by a bee, *twice*, and she sucked in a quick breath, her body instinctively jerking away. But there was nowhere to go with her arms restrained so securely above her head, and her heart pounded hard and fast in her chest as he slowly circled her.

"And this is for not allowing me to take off the corset so I can see your beautiful body and touch your breasts and suck on your nipples." The leather tip landed on the upper swell of each of her breasts—*twack, twack*—stunning her with the electrifying sensation that spread like wildfire all the way down to her tight, aching nipples.

"And this is for your worst offense," he murmured huskily as he slid that small patch of leather between her legs and flattened it against her clit beneath her damp panties. "For denying me the pleasure of kissing your mouth."

She bit her bottom lip as he lightly tapped that bundle of nerves a few times, preparing her mentally before firmly swatting her *there*.

She cried out in shock at the flinch of pain, which

didn't last long and gave way to a slow, arousing burn that spread throughout her sex and made her flesh tingle. He swatted her again, with a bit more pressure, and this time she moaned long and loud as her clit swelled and pulsed. The pounding need between her thighs grew from an ache to pure desperation. A phenomenal orgasm shimmered just beyond her reach as he teased her once more with an expert sliding pressure of the crop.

She was panting, her body on the verge of detonating in a way it never had before. It was a terrifying and thrilling feeling to be on the edge of something so powerful and overwhelming.

"Sawyer," she whimpered. "I need…" Realizing she was begging, she let the words trail off.

"I know exactly what you need." His voice was as rough as sandpaper, but his touch when he released her from the hook above was gentle.

Without her sight to ground her, she swayed on her feet, certain she was going to topple over without the use of her hands to catch herself. Her world spun completely when he swept her up into his arms, cradling her against his chest as he walked somewhere. She wasn't a small, petite woman, and she couldn't stop the mortification at the realization that he was *carrying her.*

"Sawyer!" Her voice was tinged with panic. "You

can't…you shouldn't—"

"I can. Very easily," he said, cutting off her protest. "I bench-press more than what you weigh on a daily basis. Say another negative thing about your body and I will paddle your bare ass."

Soon, she felt the mattress and cool sheets against her back as he laid her down on the bed. He grasped her bound hands and once again raised them above her head and attached them to some kind of clip.

His fingers slid in between the rope and her skin, testing the fit. "Wrists and circulation still okay?"

She nodded. "Yes."

"Now, back to what you need," he murmured, his voice coming from the end of the bed. She felt the dip of the mattress, then his hands on her hips as he grasped the waistband of her panties and pulled them down her legs and off. "Spread your thighs nice and wide for me, sweetheart, and I'll give you exactly what your body wants."

He'd used a sweet endearment, but there was no mistaking the authority in his tone, the command in his words. Grateful for the mask, which allowed her to be more brazen than without it, she did as he asked, bracing her feet wide apart on the bed.

"So fucking gorgeous," he murmured reverently as he settled between her legs.

His hot breath blew across her slick folds, right

before he licked her, slow and sweet, followed by the fullness of two thick fingers pushing deep inside her. When his lips wrapped around her clit and pulled it into the wet heat of his mouth, her back arched and her hips bucked in a silent plea for release. He didn't prolong the torture and instead ate her ravenously, pressing his mouth harder against her pussy while lapping and sucking and fucking her with his fingers.

There was no holding back against his aggressive assault, and her tense body unleashed like a wild storm. Her hips undulated with the force of her climax, and she couldn't contain the high-pitched scream of ecstasy that ripped from her throat or the giant shudders that utterly consumed her.

Before she had the chance to come down from the high of her release, he rolled her over onto her stomach, her bound hands swiveling with ease to adjust to the new position. She heard the crinkle of foil—a condom—and then he pushed her up onto her knees, giving her little time to think about her bare ass being in the air before he slid the tip of his cock along her wet flesh, then pumped into her with a hard, deep thrust that made her gasp and filled her completely.

He swore beneath his breath, his hands gripping her hips as he pummeled into her like a man on the verge of losing control. The incredible feel of his hot, thick length, along with the tantalizing friction of his shaft driving in and out of her, reignited another smoldering need that threatened her sanity.

With his knees keeping hers spread wide apart, he moved over her until his body covered hers from behind. She felt the caress of his heavy breathing along her neck, and she moaned when he lightly bit the tendon where her neck met her shoulder, as if he were claiming her. She pushed her hips back against his, meeting his deep, precise thrusts with her own slow grind, and a dark, possessive growl rumbled through him.

"You feel so damn good," he rasped, his voice gravelly with barely leashed restraint as the weight and the strength of his body rocked hard against hers. "I need to watch you come for me."

She felt him remove the mask, but she dipped her head low and kept her eyes shut. He easily cupped his big hand beneath her chin and lifted her face again, holding her in a way she couldn't escape his firm but gentle grasp.

"Open your eyes and look at how beautiful you are when I fuck you, Paige," he commanded in a sharp tone, his face so close to hers the stubble on his jaw scraped enticingly across her cheek. "Look at *us*."

Compelled to obey his order, she let her lashes flutter open. She found herself staring into a mirror on the headboard, and the breath rushed out of her when she saw their stunningly erotic reflection—with her hands bound and tied and Sawyer fucking her from behind. Her face was flushed pink, her lips parted and wet, and her hair was tousled around her shoulders. Her eyes were a smoky shade of green and filled with arousal. Pleasure etched her features, making it difficult to deny just how much she loved his dominance over her.

She couldn't remember ever feeling and looking so wanton, or when she'd been so shameless about her needs and desires.

He rode her harder, impossibly deeper, and she looked at him—at the gorgeous, masculine face right beside hers and the muscular arms braced on either side of her body that flexed with his every relentless stroke. Her gaze shifted to his in the mirror, and when she saw the raw intensity in his eyes, the fierce hunger for *her*, she felt as though she were falling off a very steep cliff with nothing below to save her or the heart beating so wildly in her chest.

Oh God. *This* was why she'd wanted the blindfold, because she'd feared this kind of intimacy, this kind of absolute connection to a man who had the ability to shatter her all over again. *This* made her wish for things that weren't possible. Not with him. Not anymore.

"Come for me, Paige." He ground his hips against

hers, again and again, ruthless in his quest to claim what he desired. His lips touched her cheek, then he breathed into her ear. "I need to feel your pussy clenching tight and hot around my cock."

She moaned, and through her fog of lust, she realized that this man claiming her in every way was the *real* Sawyer. That here at The Players Club, his true nature was revealed. The dirty talk, the dominance, the need to control were a part of him he'd kept carefully concealed while they'd been dating, but here and now, he held nothing back sexually, and Lord help her, she wanted more of this decadent pleasure, more of *him*.

His breathing turned harsh, and his body tensed along the back of hers, his driving thrusts increasing in strength and speed. "Fuck, I can't hold back any longer…"

His head fell back, and he groaned, his hips jerking hard against her ass as he chased his own climax. She didn't think she had another orgasm left in her, but she was wrong. The look of sheer rapture transforming his masculine features, and knowing she was the reason he was in the throes of ecstasy, triggered another one from her—this one deep and hot and so powerful she couldn't contain the raw scream that escaped her throat or the tremors that pulsed around the thick cock buried so deep inside her.

As the warm glow of passion ebbed and reality

slowly intruded, Paige was forced to face some truths. That it hadn't taken much for Sawyer to strip away her inhibitions and that, physically, she'd never felt so satisfied. Nor would she be able to look at him again and not think of how thoroughly he'd controlled her body and how much she'd liked it.

Emotionally, however—when it came to Sawyer Burrows—she was still a tangled-up mess. It was clear that he still affected her on a soul-deep level that frightened her, considering how carelessly he'd played with her heart and left her reeling in the aftermath of his betrayal.

And she'd do well to remember that.

HOLY FUCKING SHIT. It took Sawyer longer than normal to gain his bearings, but then again, he'd never come so fucking hard in his life, in a way that left him wasted and addicted to everything about the woman beneath him. Unfortunately, he was pretty sure she didn't feel the same. He might have been able to persuade her to indulge in a bit of bondage and domination, but phenomenal sex and multiple orgasms didn't erase his past transgression or earn him her forgiveness. No, that was something he knew would take time along with proof that he'd never hurt her again.

Concerned that his weight was too much for her, he moved off of Paige, then removed her bound hands from the clip attached to the headboard. "Roll onto your back so I can untie your hands," he murmured gently.

She did as he asked, and he sat up beside her, very much aware of the fact that he was still wearing his pants. He'd been so damn hot and anxious to get inside of her that he'd only pushed them low enough to release his cock. But she didn't notice his state of undress, because she wouldn't look his way, even as he worked to free her wrists. Where a moment ago she'd been soft and supple and sated beneath him, she was now quiet, her body tense.

The rope fell away, and he winced when he saw the red chafe marks they'd left behind because of how hard she'd pulled on the restraints—but not because she'd wanted free. No, her thrashing had been all about desire and need, not pain, and that wasn't arrogance speaking. He'd been keenly aware of just how aroused she'd been throughout each and every erotic thing he'd done to her, and how much she'd enjoyed his more aggressive tactics. She'd responded beautifully to his demands. Without hesitation. Without a struggle. Without any resistance.

Until now. Now, she was back in her head, thinking and analyzing, and none of what had just happened between them mattered when compared to the unforgettable memory of how he'd devastated her. Absolutely *nothing* could compete with that.

Ignoring the cramping in his belly, he reached out to grab her hands so he could rub her wrists and make sure her circulation was okay, but she quickly pulled her arms away and massaged the light abrasions herself, making it clear that touching her, in any way, was no longer acceptable now that they were done playing games.

"Are you okay?" he asked, more gruffly than he'd intended.

"I'm fine," she replied, her tone frustratingly polite.

But she wasn't fine. She still wouldn't meet his gaze, and he had to resist the urge to touch her chin and turn her face toward him so he could look into her eyes and get a sense of what, exactly, she was feeling or thinking.

Figuring she might need a minute alone to gather her composure, he decided to go and clean up. "I'll be right back," he said and headed into the adjoining bathroom. He closed the door, disposed of the condom, and zipped his pants back up. While washing his hands, he glanced into the mirror above the sink, remembering Paige's beautifully flushed face and the wild hunger in her eyes as he'd sunk so fucking deep inside her pussy. Remembering the way she'd screamed in ecstasy when she'd come for him that last time.

God, she was so damned perfect, and she hated him.

Knowing he had a long way to go to make amends, but determined to make some kind of headway tonight while he had her alone, he dried his hands and returned to the playroom. She'd already put her panties back on and was zipping up her skirt.

"I need to go," she said and started for the door.

In a few quick strides, he reached her and grabbed her arm, bringing her to an abrupt stop. "Paige, I'd like to talk to you."

She turned around and looked up at him, and he caught a flash of vulnerability before she lifted her chin in that determined way he remembered so well. "I didn't show up at The Players Club for casual conversation," she said with a tight smile as she pulled her arm out of his grasp. "You gave me exactly what I came here for, so there's no reason for me to stay."

You gave me exactly what I came here for. Oh, yeah, the fact that she'd just brazenly insinuated that she'd used him for sex stung like a son of a bitch. Like he was a gigolo for hire. He relaxed his clenched jaw and tried a different approach.

"At some point, we need to talk about the past,"

he said and watched that guard of hers rise even higher.

"There's nothing to discuss, because there isn't anything you can possibly say to justify what you did with my stepsister, or make it go away." She lifted her shoulder in a dismissive shrug. "It happened, and I've moved on."

He almost called her out on the blatant lie. A woman didn't respond the way she had to him, so openly and honestly, then turn cold when reality returned if she'd *moved on*. But it was obvious that after what they'd just shared, Paige was feeling exposed and emotionally defenseless. That, he understood, because his own emotions were all over the place, as well.

A sad, regretful light passed through her eyes. "Good-bye, Sawyer."

He declined to respond with the same farewell, because her kind of good-bye meant forever, and he refused to believe, or accept, that this was the end. "Good night, Paige."

Chapter Five

"I BROUGHT YOU a double shot vanilla latte,"
Kendall, one of Paige's good friends, said as
she strolled into the back work area of Couture
Corsets. "I figured you could use the extra caffeine
after your late evening last night."

Paige set aside the sketch of the final design she
was working on for the upcoming bridal expo—a
gorgeous plus-size creation encrusted in crystals,
pearls, and vintage beads that would be the pièce de
résistance of her collection—and gratefully accepted
her friend's offering with a smile. "Yeah, I don't know
what I was thinking going to The Players Club on a
Friday night, knowing I needed to be at the shop this
morning." And it didn't help matters that she'd spent
most of the night tossing and turning restlessly because Sawyer had consumed her thoughts and dreams.

"You were thinking about getting laid," Kendall

said with a sassy grin as she set down her purse and a file folder, then leaned a hip against the worktable and sipped her own caffeinated beverage. "Not that I blame you. I haven't had sex in so long I've almost forgotten what it's like."

Paige heard voices drifting from the main floor and glanced out the crystal curtain separating the two areas. She caught sight of Summer, her assistant and front-end girl, as she helped another woman find a corset in her size. Knowing Summer had the floor covered, she shifted her gaze back to Kendall, who was watching her expectantly.

"Thank you for the coffee, but I'm assuming you're really here to get all the juicy details about last night?" Paige guessed.

"Of course I am," her friend replied unabashedly. "You don't expect me to wait until next month's Cocktails and Cocks club meeting to find out what happened, do you?"

"I guess not," Paige said with humor.

Just a few nights ago, the Cocktails and Cocks group had gotten together at Raina's to give Paige the last bit of encouragement she'd needed to follow through on the invitation to The Players Club her friend had given her. They'd all indulged in shots, toasted to Paige's night of debauchery, and spent the evening talking and laughing about all the racy and risqué things she needed to indulge in once she was inside the decadent mansion.

Not even *she* could have anticipated or imagined just how hot and carnal her evening would be, or with whom. Hell, she was still trying to process the fact that Sawyer was a man who liked tying her up and got off on being in control in a sexual situation. And what about the fact that she'd loved every single thing he'd done to her?

"So, did you find a tall, dark, kinky stranger to fulfill all your dirty fantasies?" Kendall asked, snapping Paige out of her thoughts.

"Tall, dark, and kinky, yes," she admitted and took a drink of her latte before revealing the rest. "A stranger? Not so much."

Kendall's eyes widened. "Oh my God. Tell me who you hooked up with."

Paige exhaled a deep breath. "Sawyer."

The shock that transformed Kendall's features was almost comical. "Get. Out."

Her friend probably thought she was insane for getting involved again with the man who'd broken her heart, and even Paige questioned her own judgment for letting Sawyer seduce her. But she couldn't change things, and honestly, last night had been incredible sexually. While she was struggling to understand the range of emotions flowing through her when she thought of Sawyer, it was difficult to regret something that had felt so good and so right. And yeah, that realization scared her, because it meant she didn't hate him as much as she wanted to.

"I didn't go there with the intention of hooking up with him," she said, unable to look directly into Kendall's eyes. "It just...happened." She shrugged.

Kendall was quiet for a long moment, then gently placed a hand on Paige's arm. "Are you okay?" she asked.

The genuine concern in her friend's voice made Paige lift her head back up and smile. "I'm good. I promise."

"Okay. I'll take your word for it, but you know if any of us girls find out that he so much as looked at you cross-eyed or hurt you in any way, there will be hell to pay in the form of some balls being busted. *His.* I don't give a shit that he works for Jillian's husband, either."

Paige laughed, though she knew that Kendall wasn't exaggerating by much. She truly had the best girlfriends, and they always had each other's backs. Especially when it came to the men who'd scorned them. But her friend had nothing to worry about, because it wasn't as though she was going to see Sawyer again. Or allow him close enough to cause her any more emotional pain.

Kendall set her coffee cup down on the worktable and grabbed the file folder she'd brought with her. "So, I thought you might like to see how some of the photos I took of your models turned out," she said, leaving their serious conversation behind in lieu of something more fun and upbeat. "Your bridal collection of couture corsets is absolutely stunning, and I hope you like the shots I took."

Anticipation filled Paige as she stepped closer when Kendall, who specialized in boudoir photography, opened the folder and spread out a dozen glossy photographs of beautiful women wearing exclusive Couture Corset designs—hand sewn, beaded, and created by Paige. The pictures were exquisitely shot, the women wearing her corsets equally gorgeous with their hair and makeup all done up. And Paige was very proud of the fact that the models she'd chosen ranged in weight from slender to plus-size, to let every woman know that regardless of her shape, she had every right to look as beautiful and sexy as any other female.

The soft lighting that Kendall had used gave the photos a seductive feel, and the array of sensual poses she'd had the models execute—stretched out provocatively on a bed, sitting elegantly on a chair, standing dreamily by a window, and more—all showcased the fine details of pearls and crystals and other embellishments that elevated these corsets to high-end couture status.

A giddy thrill of excitement shot through Paige that this bridal collection, and her dream of expanding, was actually going to happen. That very soon, these photos would appear on her website and in a brochure that would be distributed to upscale bridal shops. These same corsets would also make their debut at the bridal expo runway show in a few weeks. It was a possible game changer for her business, for sure.

"I think you've outdone yourself, Kendall," Paige said in awe, her chest expanding in pride at their joint accomplishments. "These pictures are so striking. I absolutely love them."

"I'm so happy you're thrilled with them." Kendall gave Paige a big hug, then grinned at her. "You've worked hard, and you deserve this success, and when you have high-end designers beating down your door to hire you for custom orders and more of your bridal collection, I can say that I knew you before you were famous."

"Yeah, yeah." Paige laughed and rolled her eyes. "I'm not looking for fame. I just want to continue doing what I love." She wasn't comfortable in the public eye and truly preferred being a behind-the-scenes designer.

"Paige?" Summer parted the crystal curtain in the

doorway as she spoke, looking a little flustered. "There's a guy out here to see you. He asked for you by name…and he's *gorgeous*."

Her assistant mouthed the last part of the sentence, but Paige read her lips. She had a few good-looking male clients who'd surprised their significant others with a custom-made corset, so she assumed it was a repeat customer. She headed out to the front area—with a curious Kendall following behind to get a glimpse of Mr. Gorgeous, too—and came to an abrupt stop when she laid eyes on a very familiar backside.

The very same backside she'd ogled just last night before he'd slipped a blindfold over her eyes. Even though he stood across the room, there was no mistaking who those broad shoulders belonged to, or the firm, toned ass that filled out a pair of crisp blue jeans. He was looking at one of her corsets that was on display, and when he reached out and absently rubbed the bit of lace along the hem of the design between his long fingers, her stomach did a little flip at the sensual contrast between masculine and all the feminine, frilly decor of her boutique.

She swallowed hard, not sure how she felt about Sawyer Burrows being in her shop, but she wasn't about to give any hint of her uncertainty or the fact that her entire body felt flushed at seeing him again.

"Sawyer?" Damn, even her voice sounded breathless.

He turned around, and Kendall stiffened beside her when she realized who it was, clearly prepared to defend Paige if the need arose. Kendall knew the pain and heartbreak she'd gone through a year and a half ago with Sawyer, and despite Paige's confession that she'd gotten down and dirty with him just last night, her friend was still obviously feeling protective.

Sawyer tipped his head in greeting as he strolled over to them, confident as always. And yes, so very mouth-wateringly gorgeous. His hard body, combined with all that bad-boy charm, was enough to make a woman weak in the knees. At least Paige's legs were suddenly a bit unstable as he closed the distance between them.

"Paige, Kendall," he said, acknowledging them both. "How are you ladies doing today?"

"That all depends on why you're here," Kendall said before Paige could reply.

Despite Kendall's guard dog stance, the corner of Sawyer's sensual mouth quirked in amusement as he shifted his gaze to Paige's. "I'd like to talk to you, if you have a few minutes. And preferably in private," he added, making it clear he didn't want an audience for their conversation.

Paige debated making up an excuse not to speak to Sawyer or telling him she had nothing to discuss, but he'd always been a persistent man, and she knew a brush-off wouldn't stop him from trying again. Case in point, just last night, she'd informed him they had nothing to talk about, yet here he was anyway. Besides, with him back and living in San Diego, along with working for Noble and Associates, there would be times when their paths would cross, and they'd need to be civil and polite to one another.

He was far from civil and polite last night, a naughty voice whispered in her mind. No, he'd been hot and demanding and aggressive, and she'd thoroughly enjoyed every single wicked thing he'd done to her and had practically begged him for more. She'd gone to The Players Club to get Sawyer out of her system, and instead, he'd given her such intense, exquisite pleasure she was certain he'd ruined her for any other man she might sleep with going forward.

She sighed at that realization, pushed those depressing thoughts from her head, and granted his request. "Sure, we can talk in the back." The sooner they got this conversation over with, the sooner he could be on his way.

She glanced at Kendall and gave her an *it's all good* look, and her friend nodded in understanding and said pointedly, "I'll call you later."

With another warning look at Sawyer, Kendall left the shop, and he followed Paige through the hanging crystal curtain to the back workroom. She had an office with a door that would ensure privacy, but Paige didn't trust herself to be completely alone with this man who still had the ability to make her melt with a look, a touch.

Nope, not gonna happen.

Her large work area and the heavy-duty wooden table in the middle of the room allowed her to put much-needed space between them, which she did. She deliberately walked around to the far side, while he stopped across from her, his gaze taking in the bolts of rich, expensive fabrics and lace in a variety of colors shelved along one wall, the commercial sewing machine she used, and the mannequin wearing the half-finished corset she was currently working on.

When his gaze returned to her, she was startled to see a flicker of pride in his eyes before he said, "You have a really nice shop. I take it you're doing well with your corsets?"

She nodded, surprised at the compliment, as well as his interest. A year and a half ago when they'd been dating, she'd been living in the huge mansion she'd grown up in with first her mother and father, then three years after her mother had passed away, she and her father had shared the enormous home with his new wife, Melissa, and her daughter, Ashley. Even after her father had died when she was nineteen, Paige had remained living at the house, using a spare room to design and sew her corsets while saving every penny she earned so she could build her business and open up her own boutique.

The incident between Sawyer and Ashley had propelled Paige to move out of the estate home sooner than she'd anticipated—and away from the one person who'd made her life so miserable for so many years—into a small, one-bedroom apartment, which was all Paige could afford at the time. She'd redirected all her anger and heartache into her designs, needing the distraction from the pain and tears, and kept her focus on building her clientele. A year later, she'd opened up Couture Corsets and was well on her way to fulfilling her dreams and goals, as well as being financially independent.

But Sawyer didn't need to know how drastically her life had changed as a result of his indiscretion with Ashley, so she kept her tone all about business. "I doubt you're here to order a corset, so what can I do for you?"

Holding her gaze, he placed both hands on the wooden table, as if bracing himself for a battle. "I really want to talk to you about…everything."

And oh, what a huge quagmire of emotions the word *everything* encompassed. "I told you last night that there's nothing left to say, and I meant it." Wow, she actually sounded firm in her decision. Go her.

"I'd like you to reconsider that," he said calmly, despite the frustration that momentarily clenched his jaw. "You may not have anything to say, but I do. All I'm asking for is a chance to tell you my side of the story. If, after that, you never want to talk to me ever again, I'll respect your decision. I swear."

The pang in the vicinity of Paige's heart startled her. Why did the notion of never speaking to him again bother her so much? She shook her head of the thought. "Sawyer—"

"Please, Paige." He moved around the table and toward her, his steps as determined as his voice. "Give me at least that much closure, and hopefully it will help you get the same."

Did he deserve closure after what he'd done? She wanted to hold a grudge and say *no*, but she just wasn't the kind of woman to carry around bitterness and resentment. She'd witnessed firsthand how those dark emotions had affected Ashley—Paige had been a casualty of her spite and cattiness way too often—and she refused to be anything like her self-centered stepsister.

But Paige *did* deserve closure to the situation, and yeah, maybe it was time to just get all the dirty laundry out in the open so she could finally move on with her life and hopefully be able to trust another man again.

Counting Sawyer's indiscretion, she'd already been burned badly twice, and it didn't escape her notice that both painful instances had involved Ashley.

She suddenly realized how close he was to her, and his nearness washed through her veins as if she'd just downed a straight shot of whiskey, making her feel warm and a bit off-balance. It didn't help matters that the light scent of his citrusy cologne went straight to her head, as well.

Resisting the urge to take a step back, she instead crossed her arms over her chest and lifted her chin to meet his gaze. "Fine, we can talk, but we're not having the discussion here."

He appeared relieved that he'd managed to convince her, though she didn't miss the way his eyes slid down to her plumped-up breasts—*the shameless rogue*—which immediately made her drop her arms back down to her sides. But the damage was already done, and now her nipples were tight and hard and visible against the fabric of her blouse.

He lifted his gaze back to her face, looking completely unrepentant for staring at her chest. "I'd rather not have the discussion here, either," he agreed. "How about we do this over dinner?"

Neutral territory and around other people. That she could handle. "Okay."

"Thank you," he said softly, seemingly grateful that

she was giving him this opportunity. "Unfortunately, I can't do it this weekend. I'm leaving in a few hours to head up to San Francisco. Dean put me on an assignment that's going to keep me out of town until next Friday. So, does next Saturday work for you?"

A whole week until she'd see him again. She hated that she felt disappointed over that realization. Not a good sign at all. "Yes, next Saturday is fine."

"Great." He exhaled a deep breath and pushed his luck a bit further. "I'll pick you up at your place at six."

"How about I meet *you* at the restaurant," she quickly countered.

He raised a brow and leaned in closer. "Playing it *safe*?" he murmured, an unmistakable dare infusing his deep voice.

Safe, like their conversation the night before at The Players Club, when she'd told him that watching was safe. And look at how *that* had turned out…with her in a private room with Sawyer, blindfolded and bound by his ropes while he'd introduced her to a darker, more forbidden side of pleasure. There had been nothing *safe* about the way he'd made her come from the provocative slide and tap of a crop against her clit, or how he'd blatantly broken one of her rules and removed the mask so she could watch his expression as he climaxed while thrusting so incredibly deep inside her body that her own blazing orgasm had followed his.

She swallowed back a moan at the tantalizing memory, but there was nothing she could do to stop the throb of need that pulsed between her legs or the slick desire dampening her panties, *damn him.*

All that aside, she wasn't about to back down from the silent challenge he'd issued or the insinuation that she needed to drive her own car to make a quick and *safe* getaway at the restaurant. Or the underlying suggestion that being alone with him in the confines of his vehicle was more than she could handle. Okay, maybe that *was* more than she could handle, but she wasn't going to give him the satisfaction of admitting to that.

"Fine," she said, albeit begrudgingly. "You can pick me up."

She could swear that Sawyer was gloating at her capitulation as he asked, "Are you still living at home?"

"No." Wow, he truly didn't know just how much her life had changed after he'd been deployed a year and a half ago. "I'll give you the address to my place." Before she changed her mind about this whole situation, she wrote down her address and handed him the piece of paper.

He pushed the note into the front pocket of his jeans. "Is your cell number the same?"

She nodded. "Yes."

He tipped his head to the side, an adorable smile easing up the corners of his mouth. "Will you unblock my number, just in case I need to text or call you about the time?"

Way back when she'd been desperate to stop his calls and voice mail messages, she'd restricted his phone number. It had been the most efficient way to let him know they were done, and she no longer wanted contact with him. Unblocking Sawyer was like opening a door and letting him back into her life. Last night had been all about sex—or so she kept trying to tell herself—but this…this was taking things to a more personal level.

Even as she questioned the wisdom of allowing him to have direct access to her via the phone, she picked up her cell and tapped into her settings to turn off the block. She quickly finished the task and set her phone back down on the table, hating the fact that something so simple could make her feel so vulnerable when it came to him.

"You're unblocked."

"Thank you," he said softly.

As if he knew just how difficult it had been for her to give him that bit of trust, he reached out and gently brushed a strand of hair off her cheek, then skimmed his thumb across her bottom lip. His eyes darkened with desire, and the awareness suddenly shimmering between them stole her breath. She felt her traitorous body sway toward him, even as he lowered his head closer to hers. Vaguely, she heard the bell on the shop's front door ring out, followed by Summer talking to the person who'd just entered the boutique, but Paige's sole focus was riveted to Sawyer.

He looked like he wanted to kiss her—and dear Lord, she ached for that, too—yet he surprisingly, and ironically, respected that rule she'd established last night about no kissing on the mouth, even as his hand cupped her jaw and he used his thumb to tip her chin up so that their lips were only inches apart.

Heat and hunger unfurled inside of her belly, along with the kind of temptation that only Sawyer had ever been able to coax from her. He was waiting for her to close the distance, to make the first move and obliterate another one of the hard limits she'd set in place to keep things *safe* and impersonal. They hadn't even kissed, and she already felt as though he'd ripped away all her defenses against him by putting her in control of the decision.

She couldn't understand how this man, who'd been so insistent and dominant last night and had thoroughly commanded her body, could be so patient and tender right now.

"Paige…" he whispered seductively.

"Don't worry about letting her know," a familiar condescending female voice said from the front of the shop. "I'll just head on back."

"I'm sorry, but Paige is with a…"

Summer's voice trailed off as the strands of the crystal curtain rattled and Ashley walked unannounced into the workroom, with Paige's assistant fuming at Ashley from behind. Paige jerked away from Sawyer at the interruption, like a proverbial kid getting caught with her hand in the cookie jar. Her abrupt movement caused Sawyer's hand to drop away from her face, but there was no denying just how close she'd been to kissing him.

The pleasure flowing through her veins only moments ago turned to a heavy ball of dread as Paige slowly turned her head to look at her stepsister, as did Sawyer. Surprise, along with an underlying flicker of shock, was written all over Ashley's face at the sight of the two of them together.

Then a slow, gradual smile eased up the corner of her glossy lips. "Well, isn't this a cozy reunion."

Chapter Six

"**P**AIGE, I'M SO sorry," Summer immediately said as she continued to frown at Ashley. "I tried to tell her that you were busy."

"It's okay," Paige replied, her tone remarkably calm despite the queasy feeling swirling in her stomach and the way Sawyer's entire body stiffened upon seeing Ashley. Summer certainly wasn't to blame for Ashley's presumptuous behavior. Paige's stepsister had always done whatever she wanted, whenever she desired, because she never suffered any consequences for her actions.

With one last apologetic look at Paige, Summer returned to the front of the store, leaving Paige, Sawyer, and Ashley alone for the first time since that morning a year and a half ago.

An edge of unease radiated off Sawyer, his gaze narrowed on Ashley as she casually strolled toward the two of them, her own gaze unabashedly taking in the length of Sawyer in a slow, sultry sweep that made Paige want to scratch the other woman's eyes out.

Ashley was decked out from head to toe in high-end designer clothing and accessories, her long, gorgeous blonde hair framing a glowing complexion from her weekly facials and chemical peels. Everything about Ashley was sophisticated and chic, from her perfect size-two figure to her expensive taste in fashion. Then again, that's how Ashley spent her days—with her equally superficial girlfriends, shopping at Nordstrom and Bloomingdale's, and indulging in excess pampering—all on credit, as she no longer had the finances to support her lavish lifestyle.

"It's so good to see you, Sawyer." Ashley's sweet-as-sugar voice matched the equally charismatic smile on her classically beautiful face as she closed the distance between them. "I didn't realize you were back in town," she said, a slight chastisement in her tone, as if she'd expected Sawyer to contact *her* upon his return.

As she neared, Sawyer took a visible step back, clearly guarding his personal space from Ashley. "I've been back for a few months." His tone was tight and flat and didn't invite further conversation.

The tension in the room increased, but it didn't seem to bother Ashley. She tipped her head curiously as she shifted her gaze from Sawyer to Paige, then back to him again. "So, are the two of you catching up on old times?" she asked in a deliberately teasing tone that was an obvious dig for information.

Sawyer glared at Ashley. "I really don't think that's any of your business," he said, startling Paige with his brusque tone, though she did appreciate that he gave nothing about the two of them away.

Indignation flashed in Ashley's blue eyes, and her lips pursed, but Sawyer had effectively shut her down. He continued to ignore her and glanced back at Paige instead.

"I need to get going," he said, his tone and gaze softening as he looked at her. "I'll talk to you later."

Without another word to Ashley, he walked around her and out of the back room. Her stepsister watched him leave, then turned back to Paige with a sour look on her face.

"Well, *that* was incredibly rude," she said peevishly.

Paige wanted to laugh at the irony. Her stepsister could dish it out but never liked it when she was served a dose of her own medicine. Nothing irritated Ashley more than being ignored or not being the center of attention, and Sawyer had managed to do both. Witnessing Sawyer's terse reaction to Ashley made Paige respect him a bit more and put a question mark on what Sawyer's feelings for Ashley actually were.

Ashley flipped her hair over her shoulder and exhaled an annoyed huff of breath. "What's going on between the two of you, anyway?" she asked, looking Paige over with a crinkle of her nose and a distasteful look on her face.

Paige hated the judgment in Ashley's gaze, the kind of appraisal that sized her up and found her lacking. And compared to Ashley's outward appearance, Paige always did feel inadequate, because there was no comparison between her stepsister's flawless beauty, her petite frame and perfect body, and Paige's wild and wavy auburn hair and much fuller figure. They couldn't be more polar opposite in their looks, and in personality, *thank God for that!*

"Nothing that concerns you." Refusing to give Ashley any kind of information she could use to her advantage, Paige kept herself busy clearing off the spools of thread from the worktable and putting them away in the nearby shelves.

"I'd say there was a lot more than *nothing* going on when I walked back here," she persisted. "In fact, it looked like he was going to kiss you."

A surge of warmth suffused Paige's entire body. Their interaction had definitely been heading in that direction, so in that regard, she was grateful that Ashley had interrupted them. She'd put that no kissing rule into place for a reason, because Paige knew the moment his mouth touched hers, the last of her defenses against Sawyer would melt away and she'd be stripped bare emotionally. She already felt too vulnerable around him, and giving Sawyer that last bit of power to hurt her again wasn't an option.

Tired of Ashley's scrutiny and personal questions that were *none of her business*, as Sawyer had said, Paige grabbed a pair of shears and dropped them into a drawer before changing the subject. "Is there a reason you stopped by?"

Her abrupt switch in topics momentarily took Ashley aback, but she quickly recovered. "Mom called me today to let me know that our bridesmaid dresses for the wedding will be in next week, and she wanted to know if we could both be at the shop for a fitting next Saturday at three."

Melissa was getting remarried and had insisted that both girls stand by her side as her only bridesmaids, to represent her family during the ceremony. Paige wasn't thrilled about being a part of the wedding party, but opting out would have caused more discord than she wanted to deal with. Paige was all about keeping the peace and not making waves. A quintessential good girl who avoided conflict with Melissa and Ashley whenever possible.

Paige folded a yard of pink silk fabric, hating the

way Ashley glanced around the back room, her gaze scrutinizing everything. "You could have texted me with the day and time."

"Yes, I could have, but it's been a while since I've seen you, and I was in the area." She gave a one-shoulder shrug. "It really wasn't a big deal."

So Paige wasn't going to make a big deal of it, either. "I'll let Melissa know I'll be there." *Now go so I can breathe.*

Ashley's gaze latched on to the folder Kendall had left on the table, and one of the photographs peeking out of the file. Without asking permission, she opened the folder and started perusing the various shots Kendall had taken.

"What are these photos for?"

Ashley's presumptuous behavior wore on what little patience Paige had left. "They're my newest designs." She moved around the table, feeling more than a little protective of her work, even though these were just photographs.

"Well, they're definitely pretty." Ashley flipped one of the photos and came to the voluptuous model wearing the form-fitting lingerie and cringed in disgust. "I hope you don't plan on including this shot in any kind of promotional material or ads. Nobody is going to buy your corsets if they see a picture like this. This woman looks like a walrus in a tutu."

Paige's temper flared at her stepsister's insulting comment, and it took effort for her not to snap at Ashley. Nor would she dignify that rude statement with a response, because her opinion had stopped mattering to her a long time ago. She'd been the brunt of Ashley's criticism for years, and Paige refused to listen to her stepsister's derogatory remarks about her designs or her models.

Before Ashley could look at any more of the photos, Paige swept the pictures back into the folder and picked it up. "You need to go. I have a few appointments I need to get ready for, so I'll see you next week at the dress fitting." As a dismissal, it was irrefutable.

"I need to get going, too," Ashley said as she adjusted the strap of her Gucci bag on her shoulder. "I'll see you then."

Ashley left the back room, and Paige waited until she heard the front door chime before sinking onto a nearby stool, feeling mentally exhausted. Undoubtedly, between the dress-fitting appointment and dinner with Sawyer next Saturday, it was going to be a very stressful day.

PAIGE PARKED HER car in front of the upscale bridal shop in La Jolla at 3:10 Saturday afternoon. She hated that she was running late, which only added to the anxious feeling she'd been dealing with all day. Yeah, she was nervous about tonight's dinner with Sawyer, and it didn't help matters that she hadn't spoken to him all week long. But that hadn't stopped her from constantly thinking about him and their time together at The Players Club—and she'd laid in bed every single night since, aching for more of the erotic pleasure he'd introduced her to.

She just needed to get through this dress fitting, then tonight with Sawyer was all about *closure*, she reminded herself. It was about putting the past behind her, moving forward with her life, and opening herself up to the possibility of love again.

Yet her traitorous thoughts kept looping back around to the one question she hadn't been able to answer…how could any man compare after the effortless way Sawyer had commanded her body at The Players Club? She'd loved the feel of those ropes wrapped around her wrists and lightly chafing her skin, and even now, just thinking about being tied up and restrained for Sawyer's gratification made her nipples peak hard and tight and the muscles down below clench with desire.

"You've turned into a certified hussy," she said and deliberately banged her head against the steering wheel to knock some sense into her brain, just as her phone alerted her to a text message.

"Shit," she muttered as she dug through her purse for her phone. She fully expected to find a text from Ashley asking where she was. Instead, she saw Sawyer's name, and her heart skipped a beat.

I'll be at your place at six.

His message was short and succinct, but a dozen butterflies hatched in her stomach at the thought of seeing him again.

Damn, damn, *damn him*, she silently cursed, frustrated by her inability to truly hate him for shattering her heart. It would be so much easier if she could be cold and indifferent to him, but she wasn't one of those women who could treat anyone with contempt or disdain, regardless of their transgressions. Her father had always told her that she was tenderhearted just like her mother, and sometimes Paige believed being so forgiving and accepting was more of a curse than a blessing. Especially when a bit of scorn would come in handy for tonight's dinner with Sawyer, to help her keep her emotional distance.

She exhaled a deep sigh. If she hadn't been able to shore up a wall of outrage and resentment against Sawyer at The Players Club, then there was little hope for tonight. She'd do her best to keep things amicable, and once he said whatever he needed to get off his chest, they could go their separate ways.

It was the smartest, *safest* option.

I'll be ready, she texted back, then got out of her car and rushed into the boutique before she was any later.

She met up with Melissa and Ashley in the fitting area. "I'm sorry I'm late," she said, giving Melissa an apologetic look. "I had an appointment with a client that ran longer than I'd anticipated."

"That's okay, dear." Melissa's smile barely registered on her heavily Botoxed features—which she had done regularly to preserve her beautiful and youthful appearance. "I know how important your little business is to you."

Paige let the patronizing comment slide. Her stepmother truly thought she was being supportive, even though Melissa didn't understand why Paige felt the need to tie herself to job that demanded so much of her time and attention. To Melissa, Couture Corsets was a whimsical hobby, a small, cute boutique that kept Paige busy but would never amount to anything significant.

"Now that both girls are here, I'll be right back with your dresses to try on," the saleslady said and disappeared into a back room.

Melissa wandered off toward the case of sparkling bridal jewelry, and Ashley strolled over to Paige.

"So, have you seen Sawyer this week?" Ashley's tone was conversational, but her interested gaze was far shrewder.

The last thing Paige wanted to do was discuss anything Sawyer-related with Ashley. "No." At least she wasn't lying. She hadn't seen him since last Saturday.

Paige's phone pinged again. She automatically glanced down at the display and read the recent text from Sawyer, *oh, and dress casually for dinner. See you soon.*

Ashley gasped from beside her, and too late, Paige realized her stepsister had craned her neck to read the message, too. She stuffed the phone back into her purse, and when she glanced at Ashley again, her eyes were wide with disbelief.

"Are you going out with him again?" Her voice hit an incredulous pitch.

There was no fibbing her way out of this one, so Paige just gave a casual, nonchalant shrug. "We're going for dinner."

"Oh, you're going as *friends*. Well, that makes sense." Ashley shook her head, sending her silky blonde hair cascading over her shoulders. "A guy like Sawyer wouldn't take you on an actual date."

"Excuse me?" Paige didn't know which comment bothered her more, the one about *a guy like Sawyer* or the insinuation that Sawyer wouldn't date her again.

"Come on, Paige." Ashley waved a hand in the air. "He's gorgeous. Hot. And you're…" Her voice trailed off, as if the rest of her comment was obvious. "I just don't want you to set yourself up for another heart-break. And would you really be able to trust him after... *you know*."

"Yes, I do *know*," Paige replied irritably through gritted teeth, though she wasn't surprised that her stepsister had the audacity to go *there*, to dredge up the past and the fact that Sawyer had slept with her. Never mind the fact that she showed no remorse or guilt. "If you'll recall, I was right there the morning after my twenty-sixth birthday and saw *everything*."

"You know I'm sorry for what happened," she said haughtily. "I've apologized enough times, even though Sawyer was the one who came on to me and told me that he was only with you because—"

"Don't," Paige snapped, not wanting to hear the end of that sentence all over again. *He was with you because he felt sorry for you.* According to Ashley, Paige had been nothing more than a pity fuck to Sawyer and he didn't really like fat girls. Those kinds of careless remarks had always accompanied a sharp stab to an old wound, because they took her back to high school and reminded her of the cruel scheme Ashley had orchestrated to humiliate Paige all those years ago.

Yet despite Ashley's claim, there had been nothing resembling *pity* with Sawyer last Saturday night. Paige had witnessed the heated desire etching his masculine features before he'd blindfolded her, had felt his hunger and lust as he'd dominated her body, and she'd seen the wild, unrestrained passion in his eyes as he'd given himself over to his own fierce orgasm.

There had been no pretenses between them in that moment, and there was nothing that Ashley could say to convince Paige otherwise.

"Here are your dresses, girls," the saleslady said, making Paige very grateful for her timely interruption. "Follow me to the dressing room, and we'll see if either of you need any alterations."

Paige shook off her rioting emotions and followed the woman to a fitting room. Ashley took the one beside hers, and Melissa sat on the plush couch to wait for them to model the dresses *Ashley* had chosen for them to wear as her two bridesmaids. Paige hadn't had any say in the matter, and since the sample size at the bridal shop had been three sizes too small for her to even try on beforehand, she had no idea how she'd look in the form-fitting gown. The saleslady had just taken her measurements and promised that the dress would be custom-made in her size.

Except as Paige tried to pull the garment up over her curvy hips and ass, a sense of dread settled in the pit of her stomach. She could barely squeeze into the tight, mermaid-style gown, and zipping it up was a challenge. Her butt and hips looked huge, her breasts spilled out of the top, and she was certain that even a heavy-duty pair of Spanx wouldn't be able to smooth out the ripples and bulges caused by the form-fitting sheath.

Frustration tightened her chest, and tears welled in her eyes as she looked at her reflection in the mirror. The dress itself, in a soft shade of rose, was gorgeous—with a classic sweetheart neckline and cap sleeves. The bodice, all the way down to the mid-calf, was constructed in a high-end lace fabric that clung to every curve, which then flared into a skirt made of layers of rose hued chiffon.

But for Paige's fuller figure, there was absolutely nothing flattering about this particular silhouette. She looked hideous, and nothing would change that.

There was a quick knock on the door, followed by the saleslady's voice. "Your sister is already out here. Are you ready to show your mother the dress?"

No, she wasn't, but what choice did she have? Bracing herself for everyone's reaction, she stepped out and walked into the dressing area, where Ashley was standing on the dais admiring herself in the three-way mirror. Her tall, slender stepsister looked stunning in the form-fitting dress, with the fabric molding to her perfect curves and her blonde hair cascading over her slim shoulders in soft curls. The dress had been made for the lithe shape of her body, and she looked as though she'd stepped right out of a bridal magazine.

As soon as Melissa saw Paige, her eyes widened, and a soft gasp escaped her. "Oh…Paige." Her soft, cultured voice was tinged with dismay.

Ashley twirled around on her platform to see what had startled her mother, looking equally stunned at Paige's appearance in the gown. "Oh my God, Paige. You look like a stuffed sausage."

Paige's face heated in embarrassment at her step-sister's very apt description. She *felt* like a stuffed sausage in the dress, and she refused to compound her humiliation by looking at herself from all angles in the three-way mirror.

Melissa shot Ashley a chastising glance. "Ashley, that is not a nice thing to say."

Ashley just shrugged, a small smirk on her lips that Paige recognized all too well. Ashley knew she looked stunning in the dress, and she loved the fact that Paige would look so dowdy standing next to her at the elegant wedding so all the attention would be on her.

Melissa circled around Paige to take in the full effect of the dress, then looked at the saleslady. "Is there anything we can do to make this dress fit better?"

The other woman shook her head, even as she offered Paige a sympathetic glance. "I'm very sorry, but it's the way the gown is designed, and Paige's proportions and shape isn't ideal for this particular style."

Melissa touched a hand to her sleek blonde chignon and sighed. "Well, I'm not sure what to do. She certainly can't wear it as it is, and there's only two weeks left until the wedding."

Despite the way Ashley had always treated Paige, Melissa had always been kind to her. Melissa clearly didn't want Paige showing up wearing such an ill-fitted gown to her upscale ceremony, and that was the last thing Paige wanted, as well. A solution to the problem popped into Paige's head, and she crossed her fingers and hoped that her stepmother would agree to her proposal.

"I have an idea," she said, which captured the attention of all three women in the room—the saleslady, Melissa, *and* Ashley all turned their gazes her way. "I can make myself a bridesmaid gown, similar in style to Ashley's but not as form-fitting, so I'm comfortable in the dress and it suits my figure better. I can even use the same lace and chiffon fabric, so the color and material is exactly the same."

Melissa was quiet for a moment as she contemplated the idea, and Ashley went back to admiring herself in the mirror, unthreatened by Paige's plan to create a *handmade* dress.

"That is a *fabulous* idea," the saleslady replied enthusiastically, which, in turn, seemed to ease any concerns Melissa might have had. "Having bridesmaids in different style dresses but in the same color is quite popular right now. I can order the lace and chiffon and have it sent directly to Paige so she could have it in a few days' time."

Melissa nodded her agreement. "I guess that will have to do."

A huge surge of relief rushed through Paige, but nothing took away the heaviness in her chest or the feeling of inadequacy the entire situation had caused. She was embarrassed and humiliated, but she had no other choice than to shake it off and set her mind to creating a knockout gown that would make even Ashley sit up and take notice.

Chapter Seven

SAWYER STEPPED ON the gas pedal of his '69 Pontiac GTO, enjoying the kick of horsepower as he drove onto the freeway onramp toward Paige's apartment. After he'd discharged from the military a few months ago, the classic muscle car had been his one indulgence. He'd rebuilt part of the engine, and he'd restored the car to its original bright Orbit Orange color with black and yellow pinstriping. He didn't drive the vintage vehicle every day, but it was perfect for a quick ride across town, which also helped to keep the carburetor cleaned out.

After a week away on assignment for Noble and Associates, Sawyer was anxious to see Paige again. It had been difficult not to call or text her while he'd been out of town, a deliberate choice he'd made to give her space. He hoped like hell their week apart had given her the time to think about their intense encounter at The Players Club and be willing to give him another chance after their conversation about Ashley over dinner.

Just the mere thought of Ashley's name made his fingers clench around the steering wheel, especially after their run-in at Paige's shop last week when she'd acted as though everything was just fine between the two of them. She'd even had the gall to pretend like they were friends. The woman was his worst enemy, and even though a year and a half had passed since that fateful night, his anger toward her hadn't abated one ounce. There wasn't anything about Ashley that he trusted, especially when it came to Paige and his relationship with her. For reasons he'd yet to figure out, it seemed as though Ashley held some kind of grudge against Paige, and sabotaging her happiness was her main objective.

Now that he was aware of Ashley's agenda, he wasn't about to let her come between him and Paige again.

He arrived at Paige's apartment complex in Mission Valley, a middle-class area of San Diego and a far cry from the huge mansion she'd grown up in. From what Sawyer knew, her father had been a wealthy investor, and he was surprised that Paige had moved from one of the most exclusive neighborhoods in the area to a moderate apartment.

He made his way to her place and knocked on the door. A few moments later, the door swung open, and Paige stood there, wearing a pretty turquoise dress with a too-modest row of buttons fastening the front and a soft, flowing skirt swirling around her calves. A pair of strappy sandals completed the look, and he smiled in appreciation as he raised his gaze back to her face and those peach-hued lips he ached to taste—but were currently off limits.

"Hi," he said as he slipped his hands into the front pockets of his jeans.

"Hey," she replied softly.

She smiled back at him, but she looked tired, defeated even, which wasn't a word he'd ever associate with the stubborn, vibrant Paige he knew. Concern sifted through him. Her gaze lacked its normal radiance, and she was much too subdued compared to the feisty woman he'd dealt with at the club and then again at her store. Something was definitely off, but before he asked, he wanted her in his car and them on the road so backing out of dinner wasn't a possibility. The discussion they needed to have was much too important, and he was fairly certain if he gave her any excuse to change her mind about tonight, he wouldn't get another opportunity to get her alone.

"Ready to go?" he asked.

She nodded, and with her purse already slung over

her shoulder, she stepped outside and locked her door, bringing with her the fresh scent of peaches that made him hungry in more ways than one. He walked with her out to the guest parking area, and with a hand lightly pressed to the base of her spine, he guided her toward the passenger side of his car.

Her eyes widened as she took in the classic vehicle. "Wow, nice ride."

"Thanks." He opened the door and waited for her to get settled in the newly upholstered leather seat. "You know how it is with boys and their toys. We gotta have them."

Once she was buckled in, he headed around to the driver's side and slid inside. The engine rumbled to life, and he drove back toward the freeway. She was quiet the entire time, and now that there was nowhere for her to escape, he finally addressed her uncharacteristic silence.

Glancing her way, he took in her beautiful profile and the thick, rich auburn hair she'd worn down. His fingers itched to touch those silky tresses and wrap them around his hands so he could tug on the strands and remind her just how much she'd liked having her hair pulled by him.

He forced himself to focus on what was important right now. "Everything okay?" he asked her.

She shrugged. "Just a very stressful afternoon."

He didn't like hearing that and wanted whatever was distracting her off her mind so she could concentrate on them instead. "What happened?"

She looked at him and hesitated a long beat before she finally decided to open up. "*Ashley* happened."

Shit. His chest tightened protectively, even before he knew what Paige's stepsister had done. "Care to elaborate?" He managed to keep his voice even, when he was already pissed off on her behalf.

A deep sigh unraveled out of her, and she rested her head against the back of the seat. "I went to try on the bridesmaid dress for Melissa's upcoming wedding earlier today, and it didn't go well at all. Ashley insisted on picking out a tight-fitting gown based on her small, petite frame and figure. Of course it fit her perfectly, while I looked like a stuffed sausage, to quote Ashley. The dress looked embarrassingly awful on me because of all this," she said and waved a hand from her full breasts down to her curvy hips and thighs.

He hated that Ashley could be so cruel, as well as make Paige so self-conscious about her sexier-than-hell curves. "She's such a bitch," he said, meaning it.

Paige's brows rose at the vehemence in his voice, and he didn't miss the question glimmering in her eyes...*then why did you sleep with her?*

Yeah, they'd get to that conversation, but right now he was more concerned about the damage Ashley had done to Paige's self-esteem, when she was far more beautiful, inside and out, than her stepsister ever could be.

He returned his gaze to the road and merged off the freeway. "Did she do it on purpose?"

"Probably." She shook her head and tucked a long strand of hair behind her ear. "She had to know that the gown wouldn't work on my figure. She likes to be the center of everyone's attention, and that dress looked gorgeous on her and absolutely ridiculous on me. There's no way I can wear it."

He could imagine Ashley's glee and that smirk he'd witnessed the morning when Paige had slapped him for his infidelity before walking away. Sawyer's gut burned with outrage. "Tell Melissa you refuse to wear the dress and you're not standing in as a bridesmaid." To him, the solution was simple.

She rolled her eyes. "That is such a *male* response," she said and laughed lightly, at least finding humor in his comment. "Despite everything, they really are all the family I have left. Melissa is sincere in wanting me as a bridesmaid, and I'm doing it for *her*. It's what my dad would want, too," she said, her voice going soft at the mention of her deceased father.

He turned down a residential street and headed for the end of the cul-de-sac, grateful that Paige wasn't paying any attention to where he was going. "So what are you going to do?" he asked, curious to know how everything was going to play out. "Order another dress?"

"No time, since it's a custom order and the wedding is in two weeks. Melissa *knew* I couldn't wear the dress, so I told her I'd make myself a gown in the same color and fabric to match Ashley's dress, and she agreed. It'll be a bit different, but at least I'll be able to breathe and sit down without passing out. But I really put myself in a tight time crunch with my idea to make a gown, since I also have a debut fashion show to put together for my corsets at an upcoming bridal expo. But I'll make it work," she said, her tone determined.

Paige's benevolent nature was one of the many things Sawyer loved about her. She was kind and considerate and generous—all the qualities her stepsister lacked. This bridesmaid dress wasn't all about her being the most beautiful but rather pleasing her stepmother by following through on her promise to be a bridesmaid. He hoped Melissa appreciated Paige's selfless gesture.

He turned into a driveway, hit the remote attached to the visor, and waited for the garage door in front of them to roll up. Paige glanced out the windshield at the small one-story house and blinked, her momentary confusion turning into a frown.

"This isn't a restaurant," she said, a soft accusation

lacing her voice.

"I never said I was taking you to a restaurant for dinner. *You* made that assumption," he pointed out with a persuasive smile as he casually draped his wrist over the steering wheel. "I said I wanted to talk to you over dinner, which left the location wide open. This is my place."

Her eyes filled with skepticism. "Why are we here?" she asked, her unease tangible.

He wondered if she was worried he'd take advantage of her or if she didn't trust herself to be alone with him. He'd like to believe it was the latter, that after their night together at the club, she craved more. He sure as hell wanted a whole lot more—not just sex but a fresh start—but not until a few things between them were finally resolved.

"We're here for dinner." When she didn't reply, he added, "I really don't want to have this conversation in the middle of a restaurant, where other people can overhear us. Do you?"

"No." She relaxed, because his reasoning made perfect sense. "But I hope you plan on feeding me, because I skipped lunch and I'm starved."

"Don't worry, you'll be well fed," he said, a low, teasing innuendo in his voice.

She shot him a firm look. "Dinner and *conversation*," she reiterated.

He reached out and wound a wavy strand of her hair around his finger and gave it a slight tug, just enough to make her lips part and her eyes darken with awareness. "If you're worried I'll be bringing out my ropes and tying you up again, I promise I'll be on my best behavior, and I swear I won't do anything you don't want me to." He winked playfully at her.

"Nothing is going to happen except dinner and conversation," she said again, the husky note in her voice belying the desire softening her features.

That unconcealed longing was enough to give him a small measure of encouragement. Anything that happened between them would definitely be all up to her, but that didn't mean he wouldn't find subtle ways to remind her of last Friday night at the club and just how much she'd enjoyed those kinkier tendencies of his. He didn't expect her to make any of this easy on him, including persuading her to give him another opportunity to prove how serious he was about having her back in his life again, but he was up for the challenge.

He returned both hands to the wheel and parked the car, then used the garage door to enter the house. They walked directly into a small but efficient kitchen, which led to a tiny dinette area with a table and four chairs, then opened up to the connecting family room, where there was minimal furniture—a wide, comfortable couch and a huge sixty-inch TV displayed on a cabinet. The place had all he needed for now.

"I know it's not much, but it works as a bachelor pad," he said.

"Did you buy this house?" she asked curiously as she looked around.

"No." He set his keys in a dish on the far counter. "I'm renting the place until I find a house I want to buy."

"Yeah, I'd like to buy my own place sometime, too," she said as she glanced out the glass slider leading to the backyard. "But my business is my first priority. Once I'm on solid footing there, I'll start saving up for a down payment on a house."

Her comment once again made him curious, and this time he decided to appease the questions in his mind. "Paige...I don't mean to pry, and if I'm over-stepping my boundaries, just say so. But your father was a successful investor and a very wealthy man. Didn't he leave you a trust to help you out with your business or buying a house?"

She turned away from the slider and walked back into the small kitchen, her eyes a bit sad. "My father *was* a very wealthy man until he married Melissa."

"She married him for his money?" he asked, frowning as he braced his backside against the kitchen counter.

"I don't know if that's how the relationship started out," she said, clearly giving her stepmother the benefit of the doubt. "I know my father truly loved Melissa, but a few years into their marriage, I started to notice how Melissa frivolously spent his money on herself and Ashley. Clothes and accessories with designer labels, trips to Paris and Belize. Every day, she and Ashley would walk into the house with their arms filled with shopping bags from Bloomingdale's and other high-end stores. She also decided that the house decor was out of date and hired a well-known interior designer to help her completely renovate every single room with all new and expensive furnishings. And she remodeled the kitchen into this gourmet masterpiece that she never used because she'd hired a chef to cook our meals."

"Jesus," he muttered. "That's insane."

"It definitely seemed overkill to me," she agreed, propping her hip against the counter a few feet away from him. "About a year or so before my father passed away, he lost a lot of money on a few bad investments, and it was hard for him to recover financially. I'd overhear heated arguments between him and Melissa about her outrageous spending habits and how they couldn't afford all the excess, but it never seemed to make a difference. It wasn't until my father died that I found out that Melissa had put him hundreds of thousands of dollars in debt, and he hadn't gotten around to securing a trust for me, so there wasn't anything left for me to inherit.

He swore beneath his breath, unable to believe how financially irresponsible Melissa had been, and Paige had suffered for it—yet there was no resentment in her voice as she told him what had happened.

"How was Melissa able to keep that huge mansion of a house?" When he'd met Paige, she was still living there, too, and that had been at least five years after her father had died.

"My dad left Melissa a substantial life insurance policy, which helped to make the house payments, but even that dwindled away to nothing. I'm pretty sure that the place is mortgaged to the hilt by now, which is probably why she's marrying the wealthy real estate magnate she's been dating for the past year." Her mouth tipped up wryly. "She's a woman used to living a life of luxury, as is Ashley, and I don't think she's willing to give that lifestyle up anytime soon."

"Wow." He shook his head, so blown away that it was the only word he could find to express how stupefied he was. "Aren't you even a little bit pissed that Melissa spent everything your dad worked so hard for, which then left you with *nothing*?"

"I certainly wasn't happy about it, and yes, I was angry for a long time, but what's done is done, and I can't change anything." She gave a one-shoulder shrug, her green gaze so clear and sincere. "So, instead of spending years being bitter and resentful, I just decided that I needed to move on with my life and find a way to support myself, instead of relying on someone else to take care of me financially, like Melissa and Ashley. Besides, I'm happy where I'm at and with what I'm doing. Money will come, as long as I work hard for it."

His respect for Paige rose another ten notches, as did his attraction to her, because he found her positive outlook to be so incredibly sexy. "You're amazing."

"No, not really." Her face flushed ever-so-slightly at the compliment. "But I *am* very hungry, and you promised to feed me."

He chuckled and headed toward the refrigerator. "That I did."

"And we still have a lot more to discuss," she said pointedly.

He glanced over his shoulder at her and nodded solemnly. "Yes, we do."

He grabbed a paper bag from the refrigerator with the sides imprinted with the name Jack and Giulio's, which was Paige's favorite Italian restaurant and a place they'd eaten at often when they'd been dating. He set the sack on the counter, and she watched with interest as he pulled out two aluminum takeout containers and a side of garlic bread.

She bit her bottom lip, her gaze enthusiastic. "Dare I hope that there is veal scaloppine piccata in one of those containers?"

He grinned as he turned on the oven and slid the two aluminum trays inside to warm up their meal, then set a timer. "Both of them, actually. One for you and one for me."

"You know how much I love that dish," she accused humorously. "Are you trying to get on my good side?"

"Yes, I am." He retrieved two bottles from the refrigerator and walked back toward her. "I'll take any kind of advantage I can get, even if it means bribing you with your favorite meal and a Fuzzy Navel wine cooler," he said, holding out said enticement.

He'd been teasing her and meant to make her smile at the memory of how she'd once sipped the sweetened alcohol drink from his belly button, right before he flipped her onto her back, spread her legs, and drizzled the rest of the wine cooler over her pussy, then lapped up every last bit with his tongue. But he knew immediately, based on the furrowing of her brow, that her mind went somewhere else instead—to that damn night that was like a brick wall between them.

Tonight, he intended to blast it to smithereens.

"Come on, let's go sit out back and talk while our dinner heats up," he suggested and headed in that direction, with Paige following behind.

His patio furniture consisted of two wrought iron chairs with padded seats and a small glass-top table. She settled into one chair, and he took the one across from her.

Holding her gaze, he took a deep breath, released it, and started the conversation. "I need to tell you exactly what happened the night of your twenty-sixth birthday, at least up to the point that I remember."

"What does that mean?" she asked, her tone confused.

"I'll explain everything." But first, he had to start at the beginning.

Paige's party had taken place at her stepmother's house, to take advantage of the warm summer evening with the pool out back and an outdoor barbeque. There had been about fifteen of her friends there to celebrate her day, including her stepsister, Ashley, who'd been coming on to him since the first time Paige had introduced him to her a few weeks prior. He hadn't said anything to Paige at the time, because to him, Ashley was inconsequential—which only seemed to make her more determined to get his attention.

"From the day I met Ashley, she'd flirted with me whenever you weren't around and would say inappropriate things, especially considering she was your stepsister and I was dating *you*." He refrained from telling Paige the cruel and mean comments Ashley had made in an attempt to belittle her, because none of that was necessary and would only hurt Paige more. "At first I was polite to her, because I thought it was harmless teasing, but it didn't take me long to realize that she was serious in her attempts to proposition me. I made it clear, in no uncertain terms, that I wasn't the least bit interested in her and to stop with all the crap. That was a few days before your birthday party."

He watched Paige lift the bottle to her lips and take a drink of the Fuzzy Navel, and wasn't sure what to make of her silence. Then again, what was there for her to say at this point? Her expression was wary, her demeanor equally guarded, even though he knew none of this was easy for her to hear, and it was only going to get worse.

He took a fortifying drink of his own wine cooler, wishing he'd poured himself something far stronger, then went on. "The night of your birthday party, she was actually friendly, rather than obnoxious, and I thought I'd finally gotten through to her and she was trying to be nice. A few hours into the party, you were talking to some friends by the pool, and I went inside to get a beer, and Ashley was walking out to the backyard with two of them in her hands. She gave me one of the bottles and said she was extending a peace offering, so I took it."

He absently swiped at the condensation on his bottle, still unable to get a read on Paige. He ached to reach out and touch her hand for some kind of connection but knew she'd most likely pull away. "Before I could walk away and get back to you, Ashley asked me about the military, and since I thought she was making up for her previous behavior, I decided it was no big deal and answered her questions while drinking my beer. I figured if I was going to date you, she and I needed to at least be civil to one another. And then things started getting a little fuzzy."

"Fuzzy how?" she asked, a frown furrowing her brow.

"I felt nauseated and light-headed and very confused. I had this weird sense of tunnel vision, like I was going to pass out, and I recall Ashley asking me if I was okay, but I don't remember what happened after that. The next thing I knew, I was waking up in Ashley's bed, completely disoriented with no recollection of how I got there." He didn't go into the sordid details—that they'd both been completely naked and there'd been irrefutable proof they'd had sex. Not to mention Ashley's attempt at seducing him the morning after that had sent him scrambling off the bed in horror and panic.

The pain that flickered across her face made Sawyer's gut cramp. "Did you have *that* much to drink?"

"No," he said adamantly. "That was only my third beer in the span of three hours. I wasn't the least bit drunk." As he'd spent the following days obsessively replaying the situation over in his mind, the one thing he knew for certain was that he hadn't been intoxicated, especially to the point that he'd pass out and not remember anything.

She sat back in her chair and crossed her arms over her chest, looking far too skeptical for his liking. "If you weren't drunk, then how could you have blacked out?"

Bracing his forearms on the table, he held her gaze with his, *needing* her to believe what he suspected had happened. "The only thing that makes sense to me is that Ashley had to have put a roofie in my beer."

Paige's eyes widened, and she sucked in a shocked breath, but he didn't give her time to respond.

"I spent *days* thinking about everything…Ashley's seemingly nice behavior, her handing me a drink, and how I started to feel after nearly drinking all the beer. All the reactions I had are symptoms directly related to Rohypnol. When I realized that, I tried to call you, but you'd blocked my number, and even when I showed up at your house, Melissa wouldn't let me inside."

Sawyer was fairly certain that even if he'd found a

way to talk to Paige, she would have been too devastated to believe a word he said. "Five days later, I was deployed to Iraq, but I spent every one of those fifteen months consumed by guilt and regrets. My biggest fear was that something would happen to me during a mission, and I'd never get this chance to talk to you, or especially to tell you that whatever happened between me and Ashley, it was *not* consensual on my part."

"I don't even know what to think or say," she said softly.

Say you believe me, he thought but remained silent. He had to trust that she'd get there on her own, without any pressure from him.

She rubbed her fingers across her forehead, looking so torn and confused, and Sawyer hated that he was the source of her emotional upheaval.

The timer in the kitchen rang, signaling that dinner was ready. The interruption couldn't have come at a better time. He'd given Paige so much to think about and process, and he figured she could use some time to mull things over while he put their meal together. He knew this conversation wasn't over, but there was no sense in letting their piccata dry out in the oven.

"Come on, let's go eat dinner," he said and stood up, offering Paige his hand.

She hesitated only a moment before sliding her fingers against his palm and allowing him to hold her hand as they walked back inside the house. It was a polite gesture, but it gave him a sliver of hope that she no longer hated him as much as she once had. That maybe they could work through all this together and come out stronger as a couple as a result, even though he knew it was going to take time and patience to earn her trust back again.

Chapter Eight

P AIGE'S MIND SPUN in a dozen different directions as she followed Sawyer back into the house and tried to process everything he'd just told her.

"Have a seat at the table, and I'll put our dinner on some plates," he said, then strode over to the oven.

Grateful for the reprieve and the few extra minutes alone to wrap her mind around the fact that Ashley had most likely drugged Sawyer, Paige sat down in a chair facing the kitchen. The night of her twenty-sixth birthday and the morning after were such incredibly painful memories for her, and for the past year and a half, she'd tried to make sense of why Sawyer had cheated on her—and so blatantly.

If Ashley were to be believed, Sawyer had told her that he was bored with Paige, that he'd only slept with her because he felt sorry for her, but deep down inside, those mean, cruel comments from her stepsister had never completely rung true for Paige. From the very beginning of their relationship, Sawyer had always been open and honest with her, had never so much as glanced at another woman when they were together or made her feel insecure in any way. But watching him descend those stairs looking so disheveled, with Ashley running after him in a barely there robe, had messed with Paige's head in a major way and made her question how she could have misjudged Sawyer's character so badly.

Then again, that wasn't the first time a guy had taken advantage of her and used her. That was another humiliating memory that had devastated Paige, and it had taken her years to trust a man again. And that man had been Sawyer, which had made his betrayal twice as unbearable, not to mention how his infidelity had eaten at her self-esteem.

Except, according to him, he couldn't even remember sleeping with Ashley.

Did Paige believe that her stepsister was capable of drugging Sawyer when he'd rejected her advances? Sadly, yes, she did.

But that knowledge didn't wipe the slate clean between them. Believing Sawyer was easy, but opening herself back up emotionally and letting go of her own doubts, fears, and insecurities was far more difficult.

Sawyer set a plate of food in front of her, pulling

her out of her deep thoughts. The delicious scent of dinner made her stomach growl, and as soon as he was seated across from her at the small dinette table, she picked up a fork and took a bite, savoring the taste of veal, herbs, and capers.

"You've been quiet," Sawyer said, his voice low and concerned. "I want to know what's on your mind and what you're thinking."

She glanced up at him, seeing the genuine care in his eyes. She didn't want to discuss all her self-doubts and stupid insecurities—alleviating those feelings would just take time.

She put her fork into her pasta and twirled the thin noodles around the tines. "There's something I want to ask you about that night with Ashley," she said instead. "About half an hour after you went inside the house, I got a text from you that something came up and you had to leave." Her voice was hoarser than she'd intended. "Did you send that text?"

"I saw that message on my phone the next day," he said, his voice gruff. "I didn't send it. I'm assuming Ashley did."

She pushed a little harder, hating that she needed that extra reassurance. "If you blacked out, then how can you be so sure?"

He didn't back down from her inquisition, nor did he seem annoyed that she was pushing the issue.

"Because, like I said, I never would have knowingly cheated on you."

"You can't make a promise like that."

"Yes, I can." He met her gaze from across the table, his expression hard and uncompromising. "And let me tell you why. Growing up, my father cheated on my mother a few times. I remember the fights and arguments when she found out, along with the continuous cycle of her crying, then yelling, and my dad apologizing. My mother was hurt, and I hated seeing her in that kind of pain, but she and my father never had the kind of marriage where they communicated and openly talked about the problems in their relationship. And my father refused to go to a therapist with my mom to work through those issues, so instead she punished him."

Paige ate a bite of veal, shocked by the revelation. She'd met Sawyer's parents a few times, and while she'd never known about his father's infidelities, she now realized why she'd always detected an underlying strain between his mom and dad. "Punished him how?"

Sawyer finished off the last of his meal and set his utensils on his plate, his jaw clenched tight. "For months after each of the affairs, things in the house were tense. My mother was cold and bitter and distant with my father, even though he tried to make things right in his own way, but she'd never forgive him. Not that I'm excusing his behavior, because I'm not. He was dead wrong for having the affairs, and since my mother couldn't get over it, she put him through hell. And because neither of them got counseling to work through their issues, she held on to so much anger she froze him out, and the cycle kept repeating itself."

"But your parents are still married." Paige shook her head at the insanity of his parents' relationship as she drank the last of her wine cooler. "Why don't they just get a divorce?"

"My dad stays out of guilt," he said with a shrug. "My mom has nothing else in her life. They got married when she was eighteen because she was pregnant with my older brother, Sean, and she's never worked. She has no concept of how to live not being married. It's a fucked up situation any way you look at it, and neither one is truly happy."

"That's sad." She couldn't imagine staying married to someone who cheated on her. Then again, she didn't depend on a man for her livelihood as Sawyer's mom did—and she never would.

"Yeah, it was hell growing up watching how de-structive they were to each other and how they hurt one another over and over again. It's the reason Sean went to college in Boston and now lives there, and why I went into the military as soon as I graduated from high school—to get away from the tension and strain that pervaded their relationship and the house." He reached across the table and touched his fingers to the back of her hand resting near her plate, the truth burning in his gaze. "And it's especially why I can make the promise that I would never deliberately cheat on you. I've seen firsthand how devastating the fallout can be."

His thumb skimmed across the backs of her knuckles, his gaze imploring. "I need you to forgive me, Paige, and I know that's going to take time. I want another chance to prove that I still want you, and only *you*."

Her chest knotted at his words. He wanted the forgiveness his mother had never given his father, and that was easy enough to grant, because she did forgive Sawyer, and she wasn't the type of woman who would punish someone indefinitely for a mistake. Right now, Sawyer wanted her, but Paige couldn't shake that fear deep down inside that he would eventually move on when another woman interested him more than she did. She understood that those insecurities were her issues, not his, but she couldn't get past them overnight or after one enlightening conversation. The thought of handing Sawyer that kind of emotional trust again, along with her heart, still made her apprehensive. But she couldn't deny how much she wanted to believe and move on. With him.

"Why me?" she asked, needing to know *why* he wanted her.

He tipped his head to the side, an amused smile playing at the corners of his mouth. "What do you mean, why you?"

She exhaled a deep breath and forced out the crazy question before she changed her mind. "You're hot and gorgeous, and you could have any woman you want. So what is it about me that you're attracted to?" It was something she'd always wondered.

"Jesus, Paige, you have no idea just how beautiful you are," he said in a serious tone. "You're this rare combination of sweet and sexy that I can't resist. There is nothing arrogant or vain about you, and that's so damn refreshing. I love your curves, your long, auburn hair, and your expressive green eyes that make my blood run hot when they go dark with desire." His gaze dropped lower, as did his voice. "And your mouth…you fucking slay me with those soft lips and make me want to do sinful, dirty things to that warm, lush mouth."

A liquid rush of heat shot straight down between Paige's thighs. She squirmed in her seat, barely able to breathe as she imagined what kind of sinful, dirty acts he'd demand of her—and wanting that, too. "So, it's all physical attraction for you?"

"I'm not that shallow, sweetheart, though your delectable body is a great bonus," he murmured as he slid his fingers under her hand and stroked her palm with the same kind of slow, deft caress he'd used many times before in more intimate places. "The first thing that drew me to you, even before I saw your face or met you, was your kindness."

She laughed lightly, even as her body responded to his deliberate touches, which were just as effective as sensual foreplay. The brush of his fingers, along with the way he traced teasing circles on her palm, served to awaken her senses. Her skin grew warm, her breasts swelled, and her nipples tightened and tingled—and judging by the heat in his gaze, he knew *exactly* what he was doing to her.

She forced herself to concentrate on their conversation. "How is it possible that you were attracted to me before you even saw me?"

He arched a dark, chastising brow. "Have you already forgotten how we met?"

"No." And she never would.

Her mind drifted back to that day when Sawyer had entered her life in an unexpected way. Every morning when she picked up her coffee order at the drive-through window of her local coffee shop, she always paid for the person's order behind her—her way of putting positive Karma out into the universe, and it just made her feel good knowing she'd probably brightened someone's day with the unexpected gift. That morning, she'd received a text from Raina just as she'd paid for the two orders, and instead of driving off as she normally did, she pulled into a parking spot in front of the establishment so she could text back her friend.

A rap on her window a few minutes later startled Paige, and her head whipped around to find a disarmingly gorgeous man bent low and staring at her through the glass. His hair was cut military short, and he had the most seductive dark brown eyes and a hard body that made her swallow back an appreciative sigh. Butterflies fluttered to life in her stomach, and when he motioned for her to roll the window down, she wondered what she'd done wrong and why this stranger wanted to speak to her.

Hesitantly, she lowered the window. "Yes?" she asked, her voice sounding breathless to her own ears.

He dazzled her with a sexy grin as his gaze took in her facial features with undeniable interest. "I wanted to thank you for buying my coffee and bagel just now."

"Oh, yeah, sure. You're welcome." She smiled at him. "It's all part of my morning ritual. I like to start the day by paying it forward."

He rested his hands on the window frame, drawing

her attention to his strong, muscular forearms. "Damn, and here I thought I was special and you'd bought my breakfast to get my attention...which it did, by the way."

A warm flush climbed up her neck, his flirtatious comment flustering her. Drawing his attention hadn't been her intent. She hadn't even looked in her rear-view mirror to see who was in the vehicle behind hers. She never did, because it didn't matter.

He tipped his head to the side, regarding her with genuine attraction in his eyes. "How about I return the favor and buy you breakfast tomorrow morning?"

She automatically shook her head, not wanting him to feel obligated—which was why she always drove off right away. "That's really not necessary."

"Yes, it is," he insisted. "I'll see you here tomor-row morning at nine." He winked at her, then straightened and walked away as if it was a given she'd comply with his request.

She stared at those broad shoulders in shock, then snapped herself out of her stupor. "No, wait!"

He turned around and kept walking backwards, farther and farther away. "I gotta go," he said, flashing her a charming grin. "Don't stand me up and break my heart, beautiful."

He slid into his car and drove off in the opposite direction, leaving Paige sitting in her own vehicle in stunned disbelief. She didn't even know his name. There was no way she'd be so rude as to not show up at the designated time, and as she got dressed the following morning, she'd convinced herself that he was just being friendly and nice.

He'd asked her out to dinner and a movie for that weekend. Her nerves had kicked in and she'd told him she was too busy to date. That hadn't deterred him, and he'd insisted on meeting her for breakfast…every single morning, if that was the only hour she had to spare.

For over a week, they drank their coffee and talked, about his life in the military, a bit about her growing corset business, and other common interests. He flirted shamelessly, made her smile and laugh, and there was never a shortage of conversation between them. He'd stuck around much longer than most men would have, considering she'd kept him squarely in the friend zone.

The next time he'd asked her out on a *real* date, she'd taken the leap and said yes but kept him at first base—kissing only—for a while, and it was longer still before she'd trusted him enough to sleep with him. Even then, she'd been way more modest and reserved in the bedroom than she was certain a sexual man like Sawyer preferred or was used to. Especially now that Paige knew he'd suppressed his more dominant urges in order to slowly ease her into accepting that he had a kinky side, which she'd only just discovered at The Players Club.

"You made me work for it, Paige," he said, as if he'd just read her mind. "But you were so worth it. If it was just about your body and getting you into my bed, I would have moved on after the first rejection."

His words were exactly what she wanted—no, *needed*—to hear. Back then she'd made it very difficult for him to persuade her into a date, then a relationship, and yet he'd persisted. And once she'd taken that next step with him, it had been so easy to free-fall into the kind of emotions—love, especially—that she'd never allowed herself to feel for another man, because they'd never stuck around long enough to earn it as Sawyer had.

"So, anything else you want to know before we move on to more pleasurable things?" he asked patiently, though he spoke the word *pleasurable* with a sinful gleam in his gaze.

He'd answered all her questions, had given her insight to his own family issues. She didn't want to spend the rest of the night thinking about the past, even though she still wasn't sure what all this meant for the two of them.

She grinned at him and teased right back. "Depends on what kind of pleasurable things you might be referring to."

"Dessert, of course."

She laughed. Ahh, he knew she'd never turn down anything sweet, and she loved that he never made her feel self-conscious about indulging. "Then yes, absolutely, let's move on."

She helped him clear the plates from the table. Since there were only a few dirty dishes and utensils, she put them into the dishwasher while he retrieved a white box from the refrigerator and set it on the counter. She saw the familiar label on top of the package and could barely contain her excitement.

"Oh my God, you went to Extraordinary Desserts!" It was her absolute favorite place for all things decadent, though she hadn't been there since she and Sawyer had eaten at the cafe over a year and a half ago. "You really are trying to get on my good side."

He merely grinned, then placed his hands on her waist, and she squealed in surprise as he lifted her so she was sitting on the counter. "*Stop* doing that," she said, even as she wondered how he made boosting her look so effortless when she knew damn well it couldn't be. "And why am I sitting up here instead of at the table?"

"Just in case it gets messy, because I bought a bunch of different two-bite petite desserts, and the best part is feeding them to you."

Yes, she remembered how much he'd enjoyed doing that at the cafe, but with a fork and not his fingers. *A bite for me, a bite for him.* It had been sexy and romantic, and her stomach tumbled at the thought of sharing that same kind of affectionate, playful gesture with him again now.

"I'm fully capable of feeding myself." She crossed her ankles to keep her knees together and smoothed the hem of her dress over her legs, nice and prim and proper.

He noticed her attempt to keep things platonic between them, and she didn't miss the slight smirk on his lips that told her she was no match for whatever wickedness he had in mind.

"Yeah, but feeding yourself is not nearly as much fun," he retorted as he braced his hands on the counter on either side of her hips, making it very clear she was staying right where she was. "Now close your eyes while I decide which dessert to surprise you with first."

She heard the firm, underlying thread of command in his tone and recognized the unwavering voice he'd introduced her to the night at The Players Club. The voice she'd been compelled to obey and was rewarded with intense pleasure for her obedience. Now, she struggled between pushing him away, ending this arousing and inviting game he wanted to play, and giving herself over to his seduction.

Her shameless body begged for the latter, and she reasoned that it wasn't as though he were asking to tie her up or strip off her clothes and bare everything she'd kept hidden at the club. This was fun and flirty. And *safe*. Just how she liked it.

Before she changed her mind, she folded her hands in her lap and closed her eyes. She heard him open the box, then he was standing in front of her again, her knees pressing into his hard, tight abdomen.

"Open your mouth," he said seductively.

What should have been an innocent request took on a very naughty connotation in Paige's mind as she visualized parting her lips for something more salty than sweet. Something hot and hard and entirely, aggressively male. Shoving those naughty thoughts out of her head, she obeyed his order. As soon as the treat touched her tongue, she bit into the dessert and chewed. The delicious taste of buttery pastry, almond cream, and raspberry preserves filled her mouth.

"That was amazing." She released a delighted sigh as she licked a smear of jam from the corner of her lips.

"Mmm, I agree," he said, leading her to believe he'd eaten the other half. "And we still have four more to go. Ready for the next one?"

She nodded and opened her mouth like a baby bird

waiting to be fed. The next treat was a tangy lemon bar, and as she took a bite, she felt a few crumbs and the powdered sugar that they dusted on top of the pastry fall onto her chin and her chest. Eyes still closed, she automatically tried to catch the scraps but missed them all.

He chuckled, the deep, male sound making her pulse kick up a notch. "See? I told you. It's already getting messy." He gently pushed her hand back down to her side. "Don't worry, I'll clean up everything later. Here's your next taste."

Another bite filled her mouth with rich, caramel pecan cheesecake, and this time he deliberately slid his sticky fingers along her jaw, leaving a trail of the filling down the side of her neck.

She was startled by the unexpected sensual act, and her breath caught in her throat.

"Ooops," he murmured unapologetically. "These desserts are messier than I remember. Try this one," he said, touching another treat to her lips before she could call him on his fib.

He popped a tiny banana cream pie into her mouth and swiped the custard across her bottom lip with his thumb, adding another layer of gooey sweetness to the rest he'd already painted on her skin.

She finally blinked her eyes open, unable to stop the carefree laughter from bubbling out of her—which felt so good after how serious things had been between them all evening. "Stop getting me all sticky."

He sucked the creamy remnants of the pie from his fingers, his gaze darkening as he stared at her mouth. "I like you sticky. The stickier, the better." He dipped his hand into the white box. "I saved the best dessert for last. Your favorite."

She nearly moaned in anticipation as he pulled out a plump, red strawberry dipped in dark chocolate. But this wasn't just your ordinary berry—no, these were injected with amaretto for extra decadence. With his prompting, she sank her teeth into the ripe, succulent fruit and sweet chocolate, and there was no way to stop the excess juices from dribbling down her chin and splashing onto her chest—especially when she knew Sawyer had purposely given the alcohol-infused strawberry an extra squeeze.

She gasped and instinctively raised her hands to her chin to catch the drops of juice, but he was quicker. He dropped the other half of the fruit back into the box, caught her wrists, and pulled her hands away. His eyes traveled down to the scoop neckline of her dress and the beads of red liquid slowly rolling toward the upper swells of her breasts.

"Look at you. Such a dirty, messy girl," he murmured huskily as his thumbs stroked along the wildly racing pulse in her wrists. "I need to clean you up."

He lowered his head, licked across her chest, and dipped his soft, wet tongue into her cleavage to lap away the strawberry essence that had trickled between her breasts. Desire shot straight to her core, making her ache to feel that talented tongue of his slip and slide elsewhere. Without her permission, a whimper fell from her lips.

"So goddamn sweet," he rasped as his mouth moved back over her heaving chest and up to her throat. "I want more."

Oh God, so did she. So much more. She could feel herself falling headlong into temptation, her body's desires overwhelming any common sense she might have used to resist him, which was quickly dwindling.

He released both of her wrists and slid a hand into her hair and around to the back of her head. His fingers tightened in the long strands, eliciting a sting of pain along her scalp as he used his hold to pull her head back, giving him complete access to her throat. His hot lips touched down again, and she moaned softly as his mouth skimmed along her jawline, and he leisurely licked away the cheesecake he'd smeared there earlier.

He sucked her skin, scraped his teeth against her throat, and bit into a taut tendon throbbing at the base of her neck before soothing the pinch of pain with his tongue. Her nipples peaked against her bra as if he'd nibbled on them instead. Her back arched brazenly in an attempt to get closer to him, and her fingers gripped the edge of the counter, her breathing so erratic it was making her dizzy.

He continued the stimulating assault on her senses, until she was boneless and trembling. And when he sucked her bottom lip into his mouth to clean up the banana custard with his tongue, she felt that tug all the way down to her pussy. She squeezed her legs together, dying for more pressure, more friction to ease the building need gathering between.

He groaned like a dying man as he rubbed his stubbled cheek against her softer skin, his heated breath tickling her ear. "Paige...I want to taste you deep inside." His hands clutched forcefully in her hair, his harsh voice both desperate and determined. "I've already had my mouth between your legs and my tongue in your pussy. Let me kiss your *mouth*."

The staggering arousal in her belly coiled tighter, and his dirty, straightforward demand obliterated the rule she'd set in place back at The Players Club. Right here, right now, she wanted his kiss just as much. Especially if it came with that dangerous edge of dominance she knew he was keeping a tight rein on. That was the man she wanted the most. The one who gave pleasure and took it in equal measures. The one who made her body come alive in ways it never had before.

She knew kissing Sawyer now would be different than any other they'd shared before, and she wanted it, *craved it*. "Yes." She stared into his hungry, hooded eyes and *begged* for it. "Please kiss my mouth."

Chapter Nine

A DEEP, DARK growl rumbled up from Sawyer's chest as he framed her face in his hands, holding her captive as he crushed his lips against hers and shoved them apart for the ravenous sweep of his tongue. He kissed her deeply, aggressively, his mouth devouring and consuming hers, again and again. He kissed her as if she'd given him permission to satisfy all those forbidden urges he'd kept hidden from her a year and a half ago. It was a hot, possessive, highly addicting kiss that set fire to her skin and had her grabbing his T-shirt in her fists to pull him closer.

Then even that wasn't enough, and she was sliding her hands beneath his shirt and pushing the material up to his chest, wanting it gone so she could touch his hard body.

He tore his mouth from hers, breathing hard as he allowed her to pull the shirt over his head and toss it to the floor. Once it was off, she expected him to resume kissing her, but instead, he shoved the hem of her dress high enough to reveal her damp panties.

His eyes glittered with lust and male satisfaction. "Spread your legs," he ordered in a gravelly voice.

She didn't even hesitate to widen her knees as he slid his hands around to her back and cupped her ass in his palms. With a rough yank, he pulled her to the edge of the counter, until her thighs bracketed his waist and his muscular stomach pushed against the drenched panel of her underwear. The slight contact of his abdomen to her sex was like a tantalizing tease, doing nothing for the fierce throb between her legs, even when she rolled her hips against him seeking a harder, firmer, more direct friction to her clit.

She whimpered in frustration as she wrapped her arms around his neck and tried gyrating against him one more time, only to be disappointed again. "Sawyer, I need—"

"I *know* what you fucking need," he said, sounding equally tormented by her wet heat rubbing against his bare skin. "Put your legs tight around my waist, and I'll give it to you."

She did as he asked, locking her ankles together at the base of his spine. She expected him to align her against his rigid shaft for the pressure she sought, but instead, he gripped her backside tighter in his arms and lifted her off the counter, then carried her just like that into the living room. She was too aroused to care, and when they reached his wide couch, he tipped her back onto the cushions and settled his body alongside hers, with his thigh nudged between her legs, which also kept her pinned in place beside him.

It wasn't the position she'd been hoping for, where he was firmly seated between her thighs and his stiff erection nestled against her sex. She lifted a brow and gave him a sassy grin. "Maybe you don't know what I need, after all."

He chuckled, not at all provoked by the challenge in her voice. "Let me enjoy and savor this moment. I'll make sure you get that orgasm before we're through."

He kissed her again, this time a slow, tantalizing make-out session. The lazy, sensuous strokes of his tongue made her wetter, hotter, but at least her hands were free, and she was able to run them along his muscled back and over his amazingly toned chest to the swirl of hair around his navel. She wanted to follow that trail lower and wrap her fingers around his thick, straining cock and feel him pulse in her hand.

He was so virile and male, so hot, and everything about him was a work of art. She slid her fingers through his short, soft hair and skimmed her palms along his cheeks, his jaw, relearning every angle of his gorgeous face. Her body gradually softened, relaxed, even as desire swirled and increased in her belly. She made a low, restless sound in the back of her throat that told him she was ready for more, but Sawyer never changed his leisurely, drugging pace.

He kissed her until her lips felt swollen. Until she felt his hunger for her in the way he worshipped her mouth with his own. Until she was arching her back in an attempt to rub her full breasts against his chest, even though she was still fully clothed.

It was all too much, and not nearly enough.

In his own sweet time, he lifted his head and stared down at her, and even in the dim lighting in the living room, she could see the unmistakable need for her burning in his gaze. But while she lacked patience and wanted him *now*, she was quickly learning that he was a master at control and wouldn't be rushed. Now that he'd introduced her to the dominant man he was in private, she knew he'd do things his way—when he wanted and how he wanted.

The thought of being at his mercy sent an undeniable surge of heady excitement through her.

He raised his hand and began unfastening the buttons down the front of her dress, his expression direct and unyielding. "If you get to see and touch my naked chest, then I get to do the same."

She had no will to refuse him, and with each button he released, her breathing deepened and her breasts grew tight with anticipation. Once the sides were open, he reached up with both hands and pulled the top of her dress, along with her bra straps, down her arms to her elbows, until her voluptuous breasts were freed from the lacy cups of her bra.

"Fuck me," he breathed in genuine awe as he propped himself up beside her with his arm. "You have such great tits. I've fantasized about fucking them and feeling your soft breasts cushioning my cock. Thinking about it gets me off every damn time."

A hot flush traveled from her chest to her face. His confession was like a dirty, sexy, thrilling secret, and the erotic image of his thick shaft pumping between her breasts turned her on, too.

His jaw clenched, as if it took effort not to touch her bared flesh. "Push your breasts together and lift them up for me, so I can give them the attention they deserve."

Her arms, still trapped by her dress and bra strap, had just enough room to cup the heavy mounds of flesh and present them like an offering. He licked his lips, and she waited, much too eagerly, for him to take them into his mouth.

But he wasn't done pushing her past limits she'd never crossed before. "Now, pinch your nipples and make them hard and tight so I can suck on them."

Another order he expected her to obey, and she

did. As he watched, she rolled the sensitive peaks between her fingers and plucked them softly.

"*Harder*, sweetheart," he demanded roughly, clearly not satisfied with her paltry efforts. He tangled his free hand in her hair and used it to pull her head back so she was staring up at him and couldn't glance away from the uncompromising look on his face. "Make them *sting*. Make them beg for my mouth. Do it, or I will bite them so fucking hard and show you exactly how good it can hurt."

She shivered, knowing the threat wasn't an idle one. She had no doubts that he'd follow through on the wicked promise if she couldn't, or wouldn't, give him what he asked for.

"I'm waiting," he said, not so patiently, as his gaze lowered back to her chest.

Her heart beat in a wild, crazy rhythm, but beyond that hesitation, she recognized the longing to please him, to be the kind of woman who could satisfy his darker, forbidden needs, whatever they may be. Indulging his orders, she realized, was directly related to her own pleasure.

Before she lost her nerve, she closed her eyes and twisted her nipples between her fingers, gradually compressing them tighter and tighter, until the burning, tingling sensation built into a sharp, piercing pain that shot electrical pulses of heat straight between her legs and made her clit throb for relief. She cried out at the shock of it, her back arching as she continued to tug on her stiff, distended nipples.

"That's fucking perfect."

She heard Sawyer's gruff voice and was aware of him finally moving over her, positioning his hips between her spread thighs and aligning the hard ridge of his shaft where she desperately needed him. He pulled her hands away, forcing her to release her nipples, which he immediately replaced with the deep suction of his hot, wet mouth and the flick of his tongue taunting each of the bruised peaks. He gave both of her breasts equal attention, alternating be-tween soothing licks and the scrape of his teeth across her sore and tender nipples.

She moaned softly. It was heaven and hell at once, pushing and pulling her body's response in two different directions…pain battling it out with pleasure.

She writhed beneath him and wrapped her legs around his waist. Her fingers gripped his shoulders as she rocked against his burgeoning erection, uncaring of how wanton she might look. He rolled his hips, meeting her thrusts with a slow grind of his own. It didn't matter that her panties and his jeans separated their flesh, he pushed and pumped against her pussy as if his cock were buried deep inside her.

He bit down on her nipple, and that unexpected

zap of pain detonated the last of her restraint. The unrelenting tension gathering inside her burst, spreading like wildfire. He sucked her nipple harder, deeper, and with one last insistent stroke of his denim-clad shaft against her clit, she flew apart. She bucked her hips against his as her orgasm shook her entire body and ripped a cry of pleasure from her throat.

She panted as she tried to recover and closed her eyes to gather her equilibrium, fully expecting Sawyer to find his own release, too.

Instead, he swore fiercely, shoved away from her, and sat up on the couch, leaving her confused and uncertain.

"Sawyer?"

The hesitancy in her voice killed him. Jamming his hands through his hair, Sawyer let his head drop against the back of the couch and squeezed his eyes closed to calm his raging lust. "Give me a sec," he rasped, not turning to face her. His cock was so hard, and he wasn't ready to take her, which meant he needed a minute. Or more.

The rustling sound of Paige sitting up on the couch beside him pulled Sawyer back to the present moment and slapped him with the reminder that he'd moved off her so abruptly, and without an explanation. He opened his eyes and glanced over at her and immediately realized he'd fucked up big-time.

She'd pulled her bra and blouse back up to cover her breasts but hadn't buttoned the front of the dress yet. Her hair was disheveled from his hands, and she was biting anxiously on her kiss-swollen bottom lip as she gazed at him with a reserved look in her eyes.

Oh, yeah, he'd totally fucked this up.

He needed to find a way to reassure her. "Paige—"

"No need to explain. I'm not sure what's going on, but you're obviously done with me," she said as she finished fastening the front of her dress. "And if you're finished, then so am I."

Her chin lifted a fraction, and she surprised him by confronting him head on. He saw the hurt in her eyes, but he admired her show of confidence. Real or forced, she felt comfortable enough to hold her own with him. And that fucking turned him on and made his dick ache even more. The old Paige would have apologized or asked what she'd done wrong, but he *really* liked this bolder, more assertive woman she was starting to become.

"There's every need to explain." He grasped her wrist, holding her in place. Only when she met his gaze and gave him her willing attention did he loosen his grip. "Watching you come was so damned amazing, and I want nothing more than to tear off your panties and sink balls deep into you." Pushing off of Paige's soft, willing body was one of the hardest things he'd ever had to do, especially when he'd been so damn close to coming himself.

Her eyes dilated at his words. "Then why didn't you?"

"Because tonight isn't about sex." It was about loosening her inhibitions and stripping away the last of her reservations toward him. To prepare Paige for what he ultimately wanted and needed with her because that would require her ultimate trust.

"You could have fooled me," she replied, her tone wry.

He managed a laugh. "Yeah, well, what I want with you, *from you*...you're not ready for. Not yet."

But tonight was a good start. She might have responded hesitantly to his provocative requests at first, but once she'd gotten past her modesty and embraced her sensuality, it had been obvious to him that she liked pleasing him. She'd liked his dirty talk and even enjoyed tweaking her nipples while he watched. It had excited and aroused her just as much as it had him. And he *loved* knowing that bold and brazen part of her existed.

He couldn't wait to show her more, to be the one who introduced her to darker, more forbidden pleasures—and his ropes. Yeah, especially that.

Her lips pursed, and her shoulders stiffened, and she was clearly not satisfied with his answer. "How do you know whether I'm ready or not?"

He stared into those flashing green eyes and decid-ed it was time to lay it all out there in terms she could understand, and tell her why he needed to wait until he was absolutely certain she was prepared for what he'd demand of her.

"I *know* because the next time I fuck you, there will be no holding back on *anything*. I want you stripped naked and bared to me. No hiding behind modesty or inhibitions. No dim lights or distracting lingerie to cover up your body," he said of all the tricks she'd used in the past. "I'm going to use my ropes on you, and not just restraining your wrists. You will be bound for my pleasure, and you will willingly do as I ask or be punished for denying me. And for that, I'll need your complete trust, because you *will* surrender everything to me once you tell me you're ready to take that next step."

Lips parted, her eyes huge, she sat there in stunned silence.

He smirked. "Yeah, your eyes are as round as a deer caught in the headlights. You aren't ready. Not yet." But at least she now knew what to expect, and it was up to her to decide if she wanted to experience that intense level of intimacy with him.

He put his head back against the sofa and closed his eyes again, needing a few more seconds before he could get off the couch without feeling like his cock was going to snap in half. "Give me a few more minutes, then I'll take you home."

He heard her stand up and figured she needed a moment to herself as well, until he felt her settling between his spread legs. His eyes flew back open, his gut burning at the sight of Paige on her knees directly in front of him, her smoky gaze luring him in. She licked her lower lip as she skimmed her flattened palms up his thighs, then pressed her hand to his still-rock-hard shaft. She rubbed him through the denim material, the desire etching her expression letting him know that she might not be ready to indulge in his erotic games just yet, but she definitely wanted to return the sexual favor and get him off.

She released the first two buttons on his jeans, and he caught her wrists before she could go any further. "Paige," he rasped, even as his balls tightened in anticipation of what she was offering. "This isn't necessary." And he didn't want her to feel obligated.

"What if I want to?" She leaned into the vee of his thighs, her lush breasts nestling against his denim-clad erection as she pressed her warm, damp lips to his throat. "I want to taste you again. It's been so long," she murmured, placing slow, leisurely kisses down his chest. "Please let me do this for you."

Jesus Christ. She was going to fucking kill him before the night was through. Did she not realize how frayed his control already was? That he was barely holding on to the thin threads of his self-discipline and she was sorely testing his restraint?

She grazed her teeth across his rigid nipple in the same manner he'd done to her earlier, and his entire body jolted at the nip of pain that arrowed straight down to his groin. Nope, she had no clue that she was playing with fire, and he intended to enlighten her before she went any further.

He released her wrists and fisted his hand in her silky hair. He pulled her head back until her face was tipped up to his and nearly groaned at the eager look in her eyes. He wasn't so sure she was going to be so daring once he laid out a warning for her.

"I'm not in the frame of mind for a slow, seductive tease, Paige," he cautioned in a gruff voice. "I'm in the mood for something rough and filthy. If you're sure you really want this, I can guarantee the second your lips slide down my cock, I'm going to fuck your mouth hard and deep and come against the back of your throat. Do you understand?"

She nodded her head and nearly slayed him when she agreed to his terms.

"Yes, I understand," she whispered, her eyes glazed with lust. She dipped her head again, her mouth following the long, lean line bisecting the muscles of his belly. "Do you know what I call these?" she asked as her tongue traced those taut, masculine grooves on either side of his abdomen, all the way down to where they disappeared beneath the low-slung waistband of his jeans.

"Tell me," he said, indulging her.

Her fingers went back to the buttons on his fly, pulling the rest of them open as she lifted her gaze up to his face again, a bit of mischief dancing in her eyes. "I call them twin paths to ecstasy, because they lead to *this* incredible treasure," she said as she released his engorged cock and heavy sacs from the restriction of his briefs.

He almost laughed at her sexy definition and compliment of his manhood, but the way she stared so reverently at his thick erection robbed him of air, as did the way she gripped him in a firm fist and stroked, which caused a drop of pre-cum to seep out of the slit.

He groaned, waiting for her mouth to join in so he could make good on his promise to defile it, but instead, she licked the entire length of him, the tip of her tongue dragging oh-so-fucking-slowly over the pulsing vein running along the underside of his cock, all the way up to his sensitive, swollen head. His toes literally curled into the carpet when she licked away the slick moisture gathered there, and an *mmmm* of satisfaction purred in the back of her throat as she savored the taste of him on her tongue.

His body shuddered, and his hips instinctively pushed up toward her mouth for more. She merely smiled up at him, her eyes dreamy, dilated, and too damned pleased that she was able to torment him.

"I said *no teasing*," he growled ominously. Filtering his fingers through the tangle of her curls, he anchored his hand around the nape of her neck to better control her movements. "Suck my cock, all of it, *now*."

Her lips closed around his shaft like hot velvet— soft, wet, and inviting. His hand gripped her hair, gradually easing her head down and feeding her every inch of his dick until her lush mouth was full of him. He tugged her lips back up, gritting his teeth as she added a soft, suctioning pull on his flesh that escalated his impending orgasm.

"*Deeper*," he ordered and met that downward slide of her lips with an upward thrust of his hips, lodging the head of his cock against the tight, working muscles of her throat. She coughed and moaned in surprise but didn't try to pull back. The incredibly erotic sound vibrated along the length of his dick, and an undeniable need spiked through his system—the wild, primitive urge to fuck her mouth until he came as fast and furious as his body demanded.

Since he'd given her ample warning, he didn't hold back, and it only took a few hard, deep, pumping strokes, and the tight, constricting clasp of her throat surrounding the head of his cock, to set him off. He hissed out a breath, the muscles in his stomach and thighs tensing as heat blasted through his veins, making his shaft pulse against her tongue and his orgasm erupt in a searing release.

She took all of him. So perfect and giving, so brazen and willing, she was made for his pleasure. She was made for *him*. Now he just had to make her believe it, too.

Chapter Ten

PAIGE WALKED INTO her apartment the following Thursday night and headed straight into the bathroom for a long, hot shower, utterly exhausted from her extra-long days and evenings at work. She stripped off her clothes, clipped up her hair, then stepped into the glass cubicle and stood under the spray. The water pounded at her shoulders and back as she closed her eyes and tried to relax and de-stress.

The last four days had been crazy busy, and she knew it was only going to get worse. The material for the bridesmaid dress had arrived at her boutique the day before, which left her only a week and a half to create a gown for Melissa's wedding, on top of doing all the finishing touches on the corsets she planned to show on the runway at the bridal expo the weekend after that. During downtime at the shop, she'd enlisted Summer's help with the easier sewing tasks while she came up with a figure-flattering silhouette for the bridesmaid dress and started implementing the design.

It was a project she didn't have the spare time for. But considering her only other option was pouring herself into the original dress Ashley had chosen for them to wear, she was making it a priority, and she was actually excited with the concept she'd come up with for the gown. Just this afternoon, she'd met up with Melissa and Ashley to pick out the shoes for the dresses, a chunk of time that Paige had to squeeze into her insane schedule because Ashley insisted she be at the store to get the same shoes *she* selected so at least their heels matched.

What Paige quickly realized was that Ashley's in-sistence on her being present for the shoe selection had been more of an attempt to grill Paige about Sawyer. *How was your dinner? Where did you go? Are you going to see him again?* Paige's replies had been vague and short, which had irritated her stepsister, but Paige didn't care. Whatever was happening between her and Sawyer felt like a fresh start, and she didn't want to taint their…relationship? Affair? Fling? She wasn't sure what to call it…by allowing her sister to be privy to anything between her and Sawyer.

Not that a whole lot had happened since that past Saturday night at his house, she thought as she driz-zled her fragrant, peach-scented soap on the shower pouf. Sawyer had taken off for another week-long assignment on Sunday and wouldn't be back until Friday night, but he texted her throughout each day and had called her in the evenings just to chat about their respective days. He didn't miss an opportunity to flirt with her, though he steered clear of anything overtly sexual. It was a fun, amusing kind of banter that made her smile and laugh and feel good. The kind of playful exchanges that gave her butterflies and made her feel like a girl with a crush on a hot guy.

Their easy conversation reminded her of those early days of dating him, when he'd been so patient in his pursuit. He was being very patient now, but after last Saturday night and Sawyer's candid statement about what he wanted—*to strip her bare, bind her for his pleasure, and for her to give him her complete trust*—she was now keenly aware of just how deeply those darker desires of his ran, as well as his intentions.

When she was ready to take that next step.

She finished soaping up her body, the admission of what Sawyer wanted from her always in the back of her mind. He was asking to strip her bare, not only physically but mentally and emotionally, as well. The latter scared her the most, because it included the kind of intimacy that would leave her vulnerable and exposed, in ways that could break her heart all over again. Yet a deeper, more essential part of her truly longed to be the woman that Sawyer coveted. The one who would submit to his need to tie her up and readily surrender to his demands.

She'd allowed him that indulgence at The Players Club, but she had a feeling that him restraining her wrists was just a bit of light bondage compared to what he was *really* capable of with those ropes—the aggression, the dominance, the control. She'd been privy to those alpha tendencies when she'd followed through on her desire to suck his cock Saturday evening—his mastery over her movements, the painful grip of her hair in his fist that had aroused her, and the authority in his voice when he'd ordered her to take him deeper, then held her in place as he'd climaxed down her throat, giving her no choice but to swallow everything.

What did it say about her that she'd loved the roughness, the force, and the wickedness of it all?

She moaned as the water rinsing her skin trickled between her thighs, caressing her sensitive, aching clit. She thought about sliding her fingers along that slick flesh to take the edge off, but she realized she wanted to save the orgasm for Sawyer. Which meant she was actually *considering* his proposition. She wanted what Sawyer was offering sexually, even if she was a bit hesitant about what to expect. But maybe if she better understood his need for ropes and dominance, it would help her make that final decision and take that next step with him.

Finished with her shower, she turned off the water, dried off, and put on a comfy pair of pajamas. She crawled into bed, groaning at the time—10:40 p.m.—when she had to be up at seven a.m. to get to the shop early to juggle the steady orders coming in, meet with Stephanie to go over the runway design for the up-coming bridal show, and start the sewing process of the bridesmaid dress.

The cell phone she'd tossed onto the bed on her way to the bathroom buzzed, and she picked it up, seeing a text from Sawyer, which surprised her. She'd messaged him earlier that evening from the shop that it was going to be a long night, and she didn't expect to hear from him this late.

Smiling despite how tired she was, she unlocked her phone and read his text message.

I know it's late. Call me if you feel like talking. I'm watching reruns of The Kardashians *in my hotel room and desperately need an intervention.*

She laughed out loud, unable to resist dialing his cell phone number. He picked up on the first ring.

"Thank God you called," he immediately said. "I'm both horrified and oddly fascinated by these people. It's like a train wreck I can't look away from."

She chuckled again and settled herself against the soft pillows pushed against the headboard. "Why are you even watching that show?"

"I was bored, there was nothing on regular TV, and I totally got sucked in," he admitted. "Man, that's one messed up, dysfunctional family."

No more than either of our families, she thought to herself.

"How are you?" he asked, the care in his voice warming her.

"Tired. Exhausted, actually, but not in a bad way." She'd rather be insanely busy, which meant her business was growing and thriving. "I'm presenting a brand new corset line at the bridal expo in a few weeks, and there are so many things I need to do to get ready for the runway presentation. And I need to get the dress made for Melissa's wedding, which is next weekend."

"Are you sure you can't opt out of the latter?"

She wasn't sure if he was joking or not, but considering how he'd reacted when she'd told him about the fiasco of trying on the original bridesmaid dress, he was probably serious. "No, I can't. It's one day out of my life, and then it's done."

"You're way too gracious," he grumbled, then she heard a rustling sound, as if he was shifting to get more comfortable on his bed. "Hey, I got a text from

Logan today. Looks like I've been summoned by Queen Raina."

Paige grinned at the droll tone of Sawyer's voice, as well as the imperious nickname he'd given her friend. She'd received the same message from Raina, for her and Sawyer to have dinner with the two of them on Saturday evening, but hadn't replied yet. "Summoned?" she asked, questioning his use of the formal word.

"That's what I figure the invitation to dinner really is in disguise," he said, sounding more amused than annoyed. "It's a summons to appear so Raina can make sure that you're not making a mistake dating me again."

Dating. The word, and its romantic implications, made her stomach flutter.

"Your friends are protective as hell," he grumbled good-naturedly.

"I know," she said, smiling, which was something she was doing a whole lot of this past week when it came to him and his texts and calls. "My girlfriends are awesome, so you better be on your best behavior at dinner so Raina has no reason to bust your chops."

He chuckled, the deliciously male sound making her shiver. "And I have no doubt she's more than capable of busting more than just my chops."

"So, you'll go to dinner?" she asked.

"If it means spending time with you, then yes, I'll suffer through Raina's interrogation," he joked.

She rolled her eyes at his exaggeration, even though he couldn't see the gesture. "So, how was *your* day?"

"Long. Incredibly boring," he said of the human rights activist, Jonathan Redding, who he'd been assigned to protect during a series of speeches this week after the other man had received a few death threats. "Same day, different city."

Paige's mind went back to the thoughts she'd mulled over in the shower, and she decided she needed to know and understand a few things about Sawyer, and there was no better time than the present to find out.

"Why do you like using ropes?" she asked before she lost the nerve.

The other end of the line went silent for a few heartbeats before he replied. "Okay, I so didn't see that question coming," he finally said, as if it had taken him extra moments to switch mental gears from talking about his job to being asked about his sexual preferences.

When he remained quiet for what seemed like forever, disappointment swept through Paige. "Would you rather not say or talk about it?"

"There is nothing you can't ask me, and I'll always

answer honestly," he said. "I'm just trying to think of the best way to explain about the ropes. Nobody has ever asked me that question before, and it's not as simple as 'I like tying women up.'"

His tone was so serious she knew he wasn't joking about that last comment. The ropes obviously symbolized something for him, and since she really wanted him to share the reasons, and this was important for her, as well, she waited patiently for him to go on.

He cleared his throat before speaking. "When I left for the military, I definitely had a rebellious streak and a chip on my shoulder. I carried a lot of resentment and anger because of the situation with my parents, and that made me feel out of control and even reckless at times. Add to that the stress and anxiety of being in Iraq, always being on guard, and watching a few of my friends lose their lives in combat, and that rage inside me built and intensified."

Paige listened in stunned silence. This was something she'd never known about Sawyer, and she found it hard to imagine him as a brooding young guy. Yet somewhere along the way, he'd learned to deal with his issues and had grown into a strong, stable man. She was grateful for the insight and that he trusted her enough to share such a difficult time in his life.

"I started drinking a lot on my downtime to numb the anger, which made me short-tempered and confrontational," he went on. "I even got into a few brawls in bars when I was on leave. Thank God my buddies were around to break up those fights and sober me up. I knew I had a problem, and I kept searching for a way to calm those anxieties that didn't include alcohol."

He released a heavy breath, as if he carried a lot of regrets about his past behavior. "When I was twenty-two, I was stationed in Japan for a year, and it was such a refreshing change from the Middle East. But I knew it was likely that I'd be sent back to Iraq at some point, and just thinking about that possibility increased my anxieties, my nightmares, and had me so irritable and on edge."

"PTSD," she murmured, her heart aching for him.

"Yeah," he said gruffly, confirming her guess. "One night, while some friends and I were off duty, we went to a sex club. While my buddies paired off with women, I ended up observing a scene between a couple, where the man was using ropes on the woman in very intricate patterns. I was immediately fascinated, and just watching the rhythmic weaving of the ropes calmed me in a way that I hadn't felt in a long time. So, I asked for a demonstration."

"So, it's not like regular bondage then?" she asked curiously.

"It's actually an artistic form of rope bondage

called Shibari. Over the course of the year that I was in Japan, one of the masters at the club taught me various knots and patterns, and how the ropes and their texture provide contrast to smooth skin and curves. The positioning of knots in certain places also stimulates pressure points on the submissive's body, which can induce sub space for the woman."

"Sub space?" she questioned, not having heard that term before.

"It's like a runner's high," he explained. "An increase of endorphins that creates a trance-like experience for the bottom. If she's relaxed and trusts her partner, it can be extremely pleasurable, orgasmic even. They call it rope drunk," he said humorously.

Undeniably intrigued, Paige closed her eyes, imagining Sawyer skillfully weaving those ropes around her body, making *her* rope drunk, and her pulse raced with arousal. "And what does it do for you?" she asked breathlessly.

"It calms me. Mentally and spiritually," he said, his tone low and husky. "It releases any anxiety and stress and gets me out of my own head while giving me a rush of adrenaline. And I like how in control it makes me feel."

In control of her. That's what it would be, she knew. Her acquiescing all power to Sawyer...for immense pleasure in return, according to him. "Is it something you need all the time?"

"No. But I like it," he admitted honestly, a smile in his voice. "It's my drug of choice, if that makes sense."

"Yes, it does." Now, *everything* made sense. His explanation eased her mind, as well as gave her a clearer understanding of his needs and why he wanted to use his ropes on her. She knew he'd never hurt her, and if he could confide in her with something so deeply personal, she wanted to trust him with her body in return. There were no doubts or uncertainty over her decision, just a heady anticipation of all the pleasures that awaited her.

"Sawyer?" she whispered.

"Yeah?" he replied, his husky voice already making her restless.

She swallowed hard and made the leap. "I'm ready."

I'M READY.

Sawyer couldn't remember two words being so powerful. So exhilarating. So humbling, and he recognized Paige's acquiescence for the selfless gift that it was. One he intended to cherish. He didn't take her trust for granted and knew how hard it was for her to open herself up this way. He was determined that she wouldn't regret taking this next step with him.

The next two days couldn't pass quickly enough for Sawyer, and by the time late Saturday evening rolled around and he was standing in front of Paige's door to pick her up for their dinner date with Raina and Logan, he was dying to see her. Touch her. Kiss her. A week apart was too fucking long, and phone calls and texts were a poor substitute for the reality of being with her.

Jesus, he was *so* whipped, he thought with a rueful shake of his head as he knocked on her door... Then again, he'd never stopped loving Paige, and this time around, he intended to get it right with her. And later tonight, when he brought her back home, he'd finally be able to give her the birthday present he'd never had the chance to a year and a half ago.

She opened the door with a beautiful smile on her face and her eyes bright with joy. *Ahhh*, the knowledge that she'd been just as anxious to see him as he was her was so incredibly gratifying. When she opened her mouth to greet him, he didn't give her the chance to speak as he guided her back against the nearest wall and fitted his mouth to hers, swallowing her gasp of surprise. He slid a hand around to the back of her neck and angled her head for a better fit.

She returned his kiss just as eagerly, her lips soft and pliant beneath his. And so damn welcoming. He swept his tongue into her mouth, and with a low, hungry groan, he deepened the kiss even more, starving for the sweet taste of her and loving her bold response.

When they were both panting for breath, he eased back a fraction and nipped at her full bottom lip. He skimmed his hands down to rest on the swells of her hips, then rubbed his nose affectionately alongside hers. "Damn, I've missed you." It was the absolute truth, and he wasn't ashamed to let her know it, either.

Her lids fluttered open, her eyes hazy with desire as she wrapped her arms around his waist. "I missed you, too."

He trailed soft, warm kisses along her jawline and nuzzled her neck with his lips. "I'm sure you were *way* too busy to really miss me." Her schedule for the next few weeks was jam-packed, and he knew how late she'd been at her shop every night.

She laughed lightly. "I was. During the day. But at night when I was in bed all alone…"

The tease in her voice made him groan and imagine all the erotic possibilities. Lifting his head from her fragrant neck, he narrowed his gaze. "I *demand* you finish that sentence." He had to know what went through her head at night and what kind of sexy thoughts she had of him.

She raised a brow. "Demand, huh?"

He feigned a stern look. "Yeah, you can't leave me

hanging like that. How much did you miss me at night? And most importantly, what did you do about it?"

She rested her head against the wall, a sinful smile curving her lips. "I missed you a lot," she said huskily and licked her bottom lip. "So much that I slid my hand into my panties and…"

A muscle in his jaw clenched. He was torn between amusement and annoyance that she was drawing this out and making him so hot and bothered in the process. Since last Saturday night at his place, and after their conversation on the phone two days ago, she'd become so brazen and sassy.

"And *what?*" he gritted through his teeth.

She released her arms from around his waist and placed her palms against the wall. Her lashes fell half-mast, her gaze as seductive as her descriptions. "I touched myself," she said, her voice all breathy, as if she were actually in the throes of the fantasy she was creating for him. "I was so wet and sensitive, and I kept on stroking all that slick flesh until my thighs were quivering and that bundle of nerves between my legs was throbbing. And when I knew I was close to coming, I caught my aching clit between my fingers and gave it a slight tug, just like you did to me the night at the club."

Oh, fuck. His cock turned to granite in his jeans as

he clearly remembered how she'd watched the erotic scene between the two cops and the woman they'd apprehended. He'd plucked Paige's sweet little clit between his fingers, and she'd gone wild.

"And Sawyer?" she continued, seemingly enjoying the game *he'd* started but she planned to finish. "The orgasm was so, so good."

He ground his painful erection against the notch between her thighs, making her eyes flare as he hit his intended target through the seam of her black jeans. Clearly, her sexy story had aroused her just as much as it had him. "I want to see you do *all* that."

"Right now?" she asked incredulously.

Fuck yes. He bit back the demand, because they both knew they'd be late, and he had no desire to answer to Queen Raina. But the image of Paige with her legs spread wide and her slender fingers stroking her gleaming pussy was seared on his brain and probably would be all night long until he got her alone again.

Not to mention him trying to keep a rein on his unruly dick for the duration of small talk and dinner. "Tonight, Paige," he said on a low, throaty growl. "I'm going to watch you make yourself come."

Chapter Eleven

S AWYER AND PAIGE arrived at Logan and Raina's
with five minutes to spare. The couple met them
at the door, and once they were in the living room,
Raina welcomed Paige with a warm hug and greeted
Sawyer with a polite nod and hello. The vigilance in
her gaze told Sawyer that the other woman was still on
the fence about his intentions with Paige. On one
hand, he couldn't blame her for looking out for Paige's
best interests. On the other, he wanted the awkward
tension between him and Raina gone, especially since
she was Paige's best friend. He wanted her as an ally,
not an enemy.

At this moment, it wasn't to be. The two women
sashayed off toward the kitchen, and Sawyer took a
brief moment to admire Paige's ass in the curve-
hugging black jeans she'd worn and the fuck-me heels
on her feet—quite an improvement over last Satur-

day's prim-and-proper dress. Even the emerald-green lace top she'd chosen to wear had a lower neckline that showed off the top swells of her breasts and a bit of tasteful cleavage.

He was beginning to think she'd dressed to tempt him, to make sure he was constantly looking at her, watching her. If so, her ploy was working, because she looked fucking sexy tonight.

Sawyer glanced back at Logan and gave him a wry smile. "She hates my guts, doesn't she?" She being Queen Raina.

Logan chuckled. "No. She just doesn't want Paige to get hurt again."

Sawyer exhaled a frustrated breath. "Which isn't going to happen." He'd even confided in Logan about his suspicions about Paige's stepsister, but the aggravating part was that he would never be able to prove that Ashley had drugged him, and that irked Sawyer to no end.

"You don't have to convince *me* of that," Logan said, his tone commiserating. "I believe you, man."

Sawyer appreciated his friend's support. "Do you think there is any chance in hell I'll be able to get into Her Majesty's good graces again?"

The nickname made Logan smirk. "Groveling works really well," he suggested.

"You've had experience with that, then?" he asked.

Logan's shoulder lifted in a shrug, and he neither confirmed nor denied the question. "Women in general love it when you hang your head like a bad dog and promise it won't happen again."

"Oh my God!" Paige's scream came from the kitchen, followed by a high-pitched squeal of delight.

The sound startled Sawyer, and he frowned at Logan. "What the hell?"

Logan rocked back on his heels and grinned like a besotted fool. "Raina said yes."

That explained Paige's excitement. Sawyer knew Logan had had a custom ring made for Raina and he'd been holding on to it, waiting for the right time to propose, which clearly had happened recently. They'd only been dating for a few months, and in the beginning, Raina had been on the skittish side when it came to relationships, but the two of them had become inseparable and were clearly in love. A few weeks ago, she'd even moved in with Logan, so it wasn't a surprise that Logan had popped the question.

"I'm really happy for you," Sawyer said sincerely and gave his friend a bro-like pat on the back. "Congrats, man."

"Thanks. Raina must be showing Paige the huge rock I bought for her," he said, puffing his chest out like a proud peacock. "I figured if she was going to say yes to my marriage proposal, then I wanted to make sure that any guy within a five-mile radius could see that ring on her finger."

Sawyer raised a brow. "A tad possessive, huh?"

"Whatever," Logan said, not the least bit offended by Sawyer's comment. "She's mine, and I want to make sure everyone knows it."

"Lucky bastard," Sawyer muttered, because it was true. Despite Raina's aversion to *him*, she was Logan's perfect match.

They headed toward the women's voices. They entered the kitchen, and Logan veered toward the refrigerator while Sawyer deliberately walked toward Raina. As he neared, her expression turned wary.

"I hear congratulations are in order," he said and prayed she wouldn't kick him in the nuts as he wrapped her in a warm hug she had no time to plan for or rebuff. "I'm very happy for both of you."

Raina stiffened in surprise but then hugged him back. When they pulled apart, she actually looked...*flustered* that he'd extended such a kind gesture. Mission accomplished, Sawyer thought, hiding his grin. He didn't want Raina to think he was a complete caveman or asshole.

"Umm, thank you," she said, then turned and busied herself pouring two glasses of wine.

Logan twisted the cap off a beer and handed it to Sawyer, then did the same for himself. "Come on, let's go fire up the barbeque so I can get the chicken on the grill."

Sawyer followed Logan to the patio and the huge outdoor grilling station that was nearly as big as the inside kitchen, with granite counters, a refrigerator, and a built-in smoker. The women joined them a few minutes later and settled into the nearby wicker chairs.

"So, have you two set a wedding date yet?" Paige asked, her voice infused with excitement.

"I just got the ring on her finger," Logan said playfully as he scrubbed down the grates on the grill. "Don't make her panic by talking wedding plans."

"I'm *fine*," Raina told her new fiancé with an affectionate smile before turning back to Paige. "I did accept his proposal, but we're in no rush to get married."

"Speak for yourself, sugar," Logan butted in as he placed a marinated chicken breast on the sizzling grill.

Raina rolled her eyes. "Okay, if Logan had *his* way, he'd whisk me to the nearest courthouse and marry me right now, but I want a long engagement."

"Have you forgotten how persuasive I can be?" Logan asked with a grin.

"Not to mention pushy and bossy and controlling—"

"And you *love* those qualities about me," Logan said, pointing the tongs at her.

"Maybe. A little," Raina murmured and gave Logan an intimate look as she took a drink of her wine. "Depending on the time and place…"

"Tonight, and the bedroom," Logan responded without missing a beat, making Raina's face flush. "You'll learn a whole new meaning to pushy, bossy, and controlling."

Paige laughed. "Oh my God, you two! Would you like Sawyer and me to leave so you guys can get down and dirty?"

"Yes," Logan joked, just as Raina said an emphatic, "No!"

Raina shook her head at Logan, then started discussing the upcoming bridal expo with Paige, while Sawyer and Logan talked shop and their recent jobs at Noble and Associates. After two weeks in a row on out-of-town security, Sawyer was glad his new assignments were here in the city.

A short time later, Raina stood up and carried the two wineglasses into the house, most likely to refill them. Realizing she was going to be alone for a short time, which would enable him to speak to her without anyone around, Sawyer glanced at Logan's empty beer bottle and said, "I'm going to get me another beer. You want one?"

"Oh, yeah, sure," Logan said as he continued turning the chicken breasts over.

Sawyer grabbed Logan's bottle and took them both into the kitchen, where Raina was struggling to uncork the bottle of wine, her back to him.

"Need some help with that?" he asked as he put the beer bottles in the recycle bin under the sink.

She jumped—clearly, he'd startled her—then she turned around, handing him the corkscrew and bottle. "Yeah, that would be great."

An awkward silence ensued as he worked the cork out of the neck. When it finally popped out, he set the items on the counter next to the wineglasses and spoke before he lost the opportunity. "Hey, Raina, can I talk to you for a few minutes?"

She met his gaze. The wariness he'd seen earlier was still there but not as prominent. "Sure."

Okay, at least she hadn't flat-out refused him, as he'd half expected. "I just wanted to let you know that my feelings for Paige are real, and while I know I have a lot of things to make up for because of what happened in the past, I really want things to work out between her and me."

She crossed her arms over her chest, her chin lifting a fraction. "Why?"

"Why...*what?*" he asked, confused as to what part of his comment she was referring to.

"Why do you want things to work out with Paige?" she asked, straight up. "Because you pretty much devastated her a year and a half ago."

God, he swore that indiscretion would forever be the bane of his existence. Like a dark cloud that followed him everywhere, and the only thing that would chase it away was Paige's forgiveness, which he knew he hadn't yet earned. "What happened with Ashley wasn't something I did willingly," he said, trying not to sound defensive.

Raina's expression softened a fraction but not enough. "Paige told me about Ashley possibly slipping you a roofie."

He leaned his hip against the counter and wondered if that was doubt he heard in Raina's voice. "And you don't believe it?"

"Actually, I do." Her lips pursed in disgust. "Ashley is that much of a bitch, and it certainly isn't the first time she's done something so horrible to Paige and destroyed her self-esteem. Except this time, it was so much worse."

Worse than what? Sawyer wondered. He felt his chest tighten protectively, and his fingers curled into a fist. "What else has Ashley done to Paige?"

Raina hesitated a moment, as if she was considering whether or not to tell him the story. "You know what? It's not my place to say. Just know that Paige has every reason not to trust a guy's motives when it comes to liking her or dating her."

Jesus, how could Raina drop such a bombshell on him and not give him details? He respected the fact that *she* was protecting her best friend, and it wasn't as though he could outright ask Paige without making Raina look like she'd spilled secrets. But not knowing was going to eat away at him.

"You didn't answer my question," Raina said as she picked up the wine bottle and refilled the glasses. "Why do you want things to work out with Paige?"

The answer was simple. "Because I love her."

Raina shot him an incredulous look.

"I dated Paige for six weeks the first time," he said, explaining *his* truth when it came to Paige. "And I knew then that I was falling in love with her. That never went away, and being with her again has only confirmed those feelings."

Raina continued staring at him for a long, silent moment before speaking again, her expression unreadable. "Have you told Paige?"

He shook his head. "No."

"Why not?"

"Because she's not ready to hear it or believe it."

Raina nodded her agreement. "Yeah, that might take her a while. You did break her heart."

"Not intentionally," he reminded the other woman.

She inclined her head in acknowledgement. "I really do think you're a good guy, so be patient with Paige. She's worth it."

"I already know that."

"And don't *even* give me a reason to kick your ass," she said, shaking a finger at him.

He caught a smile on Raina's lips, and while he didn't doubt that she was serious about the ass kicking, he knew that he at least finally had her as an ally.

Chapter Twelve

"WELL, THAT WAS a nice evening," Paige said with a happy sigh as she rested her head against the passenger seat in Sawyer's car as they headed back to her place. Considering how cool Raina had been when they'd arrived, it had gone much better than Paige had anticipated.

"Yeah, it was fun," he admitted and smiled over at her before glancing at the road again.

In the dark interior of the vehicle, she took in Sawyer's strong profile, illuminated by the headlights of oncoming cars. It was true that they'd had fun, that the evening had been full of teasing and laughter and amusing stories, as a result of a definite shift in attitude between Raina and Sawyer when they'd returned from the kitchen after getting a refill on their drinks. The tension between them had been curiously gone, and Paige had spent a good part of the night wondering how that had come to be.

"You were in the kitchen with Raina for a while," she said, not needing to specify *when* since the two of them had only been alone together that one time. "What were the two of you talking about?"

"I was groveling and begging for her forgiveness." Humor laced his deep voice.

She laughed. "Must have been a whole lot of groveling, because you were in there for a long time." Certainly longer than it took to refill two wineglasses and grab two beers. "I was just about ready to go inside to make sure that you were okay," she teased.

"I was fine," he reassured her as he placed a hand on her jean-clad thigh. "Beneath all that hissing, Queen Raina is a pussycat."

Paige smiled at that image. "With very sharp claws when needed."

"Not a scratch on me," he bragged.

"Hmmm." She let her voice drop to a sultry pitch. "I might have to strip you naked and check *everywhere*, just to be sure."

He turned his head, his gaze hot as it met hers. "I think *you'll* be the one stripping naked. You owe me a peep show."

Heat flashed across her skin at the reminder of how she'd taunted and teased him with her little masturbating fantasy. She knew exactly how this evening was going to end, had been anticipating it since they'd left her place earlier. Sex with Sawyer, and the thought made her entire body hum with anticipation.

When they arrived at her complex, Sawyer got out of the car and retrieved a rather large white box adorned with a big purple bow from the trunk, then met up with her by the passenger side.

She tipped her head curiously as they walked toward her apartment. "What's that?"

"It's the twenty-sixth birthday present that I bought for you but never had the chance to give you."

Oh. The fact that he still had the gift, despite everything that had happened between them, made her melt inside. "You kept it all this time?" she asked in disbelief.

"I was hopeful I'd be able to give it to you someday," he said, his gaze flickering with an emotion that made Paige's heart skip a beat. "I put it in storage with the rest of my personal things to keep it safe while I was in Iraq."

She unlocked the door and walked inside her place, with Sawyer following behind. She wasn't sure what to make of that, but the one thing it did tell her was that whatever was inside the box was important enough to Sawyer that he'd hadn't parted with it.

She was suddenly dying to know what was beneath

the lid. "Can I open it?" she asked anxiously, feeling like a kid on Christmas morning.

"*After* my peep show," he said as he grabbed one of the chairs from her dinette set with his free hand and carried it into her bedroom.

She trailed behind him. He set the chair down by the side of the bed and placed the present on the mattress, then turned on *all* the lights in the room, leaving no romantic shadows to conceal her imperfections and flaws. *No hiding behind modesty or inhibitions. No dim lights or distracting lingerie to cover up your body.* He'd warned her. She'd told him she was ready, but now that she was faced with the reality, she felt frozen to the spot and was questioning her decision.

Turning around to face her, he pulled off his shirt and tossed it aside, revealing the hard, chiseled planes of his chest and abdomen. He toed off his shoes and removed his socks, then sat down in the chair with just his jeans on. He flattened his palms on his thighs, looking like a king on a throne—a devastatingly sexy king who was determined to get his way.

"Take off your clothes, Paige," he said, his voice soft but unyielding. "*All* of them."

He wasn't going to let her back down or renege on her promise that she was ready for this. She swallowed hard to ease the sudden dryness in her mouth and pushed away those insecurities trying to claw their way to the surface and started with her heels, taking them off one by one and kicking them out of the way. It was easier not to look at him, to just concentrate on the task at hand, so that's what she did.

Her stomach was a jumble of nerves as she peeled her top over her head and dropped it to the floor, then unfastened her jeans and shimmied them over her hips and down her legs. Down to her bra and panties, the last of her armor, she hesitated for a moment.

"*Everything*, Paige," he said, much more sternly this time.

Something warm and liquid stirred in her belly at his direct order. Staring at the carpet, she released the catch at the back of her bra and let it slide down her arms and off, feeling the heavy weight of her breasts bounce as they settled. Another deep breath, and as if ripping off the last of a Band-aid, she quickly pushed her panties down her legs, stepped out of them, and straightened again. *Done.*

The deep, dark groan of appreciation that rumbled up from Sawyer's chest made her nerve endings tingle, and she couldn't stop herself from finally glancing up at him. He was looking at her, *devouring* her with his molten gaze, and it was that pure, unadulterated heat in his eyes that dissolved the last of her doubts and uncertainties. There was no way a man could fake that kind of lust, and it started a fire in her belly like nothing she'd ever felt before.

He abruptly stood and shucked his jeans and briefs, then retrieved a condom from the pocket of his pants. "I thought I could keep my jeans on, but there is no fucking way I'm going to be able to watch you touch yourself and not be inside of you at the same time," he said as he rolled the protection down his thick erection.

The realization that she'd driven him to this extreme was a heady feeling, and she embraced it.

He sat back down. "Come here," he said, and she didn't hesitate to walk toward him.

She stopped between his widespread legs and lost her breath when he leaned forward and pressed a hot, damp, open-mouthed kiss to her soft stomach while his fingers lightly trailed up and down the outsides of her thighs. His lips moved slowly upward until he reached her breasts. He licked each of her nipples, flicked them hard with the tip of his tongue, then bit down just hard enough to give her that rush of pain-pleasure she was coming to expect and enjoy. She threaded her fingers through his hair, shivering as goose bumps broke out on her skin, and a slick moisture pooled between her legs.

He turned her around so she was facing away from him. "Sit on my cock, just like this." Sliding the tip of his shaft through her wet folds, he positioned the head against her entrance as she lowered herself to his lap, until he was seated deep inside her body, filling her so full she couldn't help the moan of pleasure that escaped her lips.

He pushed her hair away from one side of her neck and breathed in her ear. "Look straight ahead, into the mirror," he said as he used his feet against the inside of hers to spread her legs far, far apart.

She glanced up at their reflection, only a few feet away—Sawyer sitting behind her with his cock buried so deep inside her, and her thighs open indecently wide so he could see *everything*. She'd been so caught in her own head and worried about stripping for him that she didn't even realize, until this moment, that he'd positioned the chair to face her dresser that had an attached mirror. There was no looking away, no escaping their images or the soft curves of her body, her voluptuous breasts…

Sawyer met her gaze in the mirror, his filled with so much sin. "This is the perfect position to watch you touch your gorgeous pussy and make yourself come."

Clever, devious man.

"Show me," he urged and nipped at her earlobe.

Her breasts tingled and swelled at that playful bite, and her clit throbbed. Suddenly feeling daring and wanting to tempt Sawyer to lose a bit of that iron control of his, she slid her hand down her stomach and grazed her fingertips along her exposed flesh. She was already slick with desire, and she spread the moisture all the way up to the hood of her sex, dragging her fingers through her slit slowly and leisurely. She circled the small, pink, nerve-laden bud, rubbed that knot of flesh a little harder, just how she liked, and moaned softly.

"That is so fucking hot," he said against the side of her neck, his smoky brown eyes watching her so intently, adding to the slow burn sluicing through her veins.

"I need more," she said, aching to feel his hands on her. "Touch my breasts. *Please.*"

His big hands came around, cupping and squeezing the mounds in his palms. Fondling them so skillfully. He brushed his thumbs across her nipples, tightening them into tight, needy peaks before he caught them between his fingers. He pinched and pulled, *hard*, and the illicit sensation shot a blast of sizzling heat down her belly and between her thighs.

She cried out at the delicious shock of it and wriggled desperately on his cock as her own fingers moved faster over her clit. He released a low, growling sound from behind her, his body too restrained despite how his shaft stretched her wide inside, filling her but not moving.

His self-discipline drove her crazy when she was

feeling so wild, so close to coming. Her gaze locked helplessly on his in the mirror, her skin flushing with desire, her heart racing as her release built and built. She lifted her arm, curling her free hand around the back of his neck, using it as leverage to arch her body on his, to rock and grind on his lap, on his cock.

He tweaked her nipples one more time, shooting her off like a rocket. Her head fell back on his shoulder as her body jolted, tightened, and bucked. Her pussy clenched on his erection, then began to pulsate, milking him.

"*Sawyer!*" She screamed his name, her stroking fingers taking her over the sharp edge and straight into ecstasy.

She heard him curse, then his hands were gripping her hips hard, guiding them as he rammed into her with deep thrusts, his control finally splintering. He shuddered behind her and came on a guttural groan.

A few moments later, after they'd both caught their breath, he wrapped one of his strong arms around her waist and tangled the fingers of his other hand in her hair, turning her head toward his. His mouth touched down on hers, and her lips automatically parted, welcoming the sweep of his tongue as they indulged in a slow, unhurried kiss that made her feel so desirable and cherished.

After a short while, he ended the kiss and guided

her gaze back to their reflections. "Look at you, Paige," he murmured huskily. "Look at how beautiful and sexy you are like this."

She couldn't deny that she did look soft, sensual, sated. Her skin was flushed with passion, her eyes glazed with bliss, her expression replete. Letting go of her inhibitions and squashing the insecure thoughts in her head had allowed her to focus on her pleasure, and his, and the results had been stunning.

"Would you like to open your birthday present now?" he whispered in her ear.

She smiled, still incredibly curious to find out what was in that box on the bed. "Yes."

They separated and stood. "Give me a sec," Sawyer said as he headed toward the adjoining bathroom, grabbing his jeans from the floor on the way.

She couldn't help but stare at his bare ass as he walked away, and after he closed the door, she picked up his T-shirt from the floor and put it on. When he returned, he was wearing his jeans and she was kneeling on the bed by the present.

He eyed the soft cotton now covering her body. "I don't know why you bothered putting my shirt on," he mused. "I'm not done with you yet."

She wasn't *that* comfortable strutting around in the nude like he was, and besides, she pointed out the obvious. "Then why did you put your jeans back on?"

A naughty smirk curved his mouth. "It's going to help keep my dick under control around you. What we just did took the edge off so I can concentrate on what's next."

She tipped her head, regarding him curiously as he stopped in front of the bed near her. "Concentrate? On what?"

"What's in that box," he said, giving nothing away as he crossed his arms over his chest. "If you like my present, I don't want a raging hard-on distracting me from using it on you."

She laughed, though she had no clue what he'd bought for her. But if it led to them doing dirty things together… "I think I'm going to like this gift."

"I hope so," he said softly, his expression suddenly serious. "Open it and let's find out."

Not sure what to make of his guarded features when she'd never seen him less than confident, she untied the bow and lifted the lid on the tall box. Her stomach tumbled with anticipation when she saw what was inside—what seemed like an endless coil of rope, similar in type and diameter to the one he'd used on her at The Players Club. But instead of red in color, these were a deep, dark purple.

"It's your favorite color," he said, his tone wry.

The fact that he'd put that much thought into the purchase made the gift that much more personal. She lifted her gaze to him, stunned by the realization that her twenty-sixth birthday could have, and should have, ended much differently. "You bought this a year and a half ago?"

He nodded. "Yes. If you were willing, I was going to show you how good it felt to let me be in complete control of your pleasure."

Something so special and intimate had been stolen from her, but she wasn't going to dwell on the past any longer. And she wasn't all that certain if she would have been ready back then for that kind of power exchange, not like she was prepared to cede that control to him tonight.

"I want you to show me *now*, Sawyer," she said, moving off the bed to stand next to him. She lifted a hand to his face and rested her palm against his lightly stubbled cheek, wanting him to see the sincerity, the desire for this in her gaze. "Show me how good it feels to let you be in control of my pleasure with these ropes, and for you to take what you need."

His strong body shuddered at *her* gift to him, and he placed a hand gently over hers, as if savoring her touch. "I need you to understand that this can get intense, especially for you since you've never been tied up like this before. If you feel anxious at any point, just say *red,* and I'll stop immediately."

"I trust you." Stepping back, she reached for the

hem of his T-shirt, pulled it over her head, and dropped it to the floor. She shivered as his jaw clenched and his smoldering gaze raked over her, making her feel so feminine and, yes, beautiful. "I want this," she told him. "I want this with *you*."

He groaned, the low sound infused with gratitude. In the next instant, his entire demeanor changed, and that darker, more aggressive man appeared. There was no apprehension for Paige, just a secret thrill that curled low in her belly.

"Stand in front of the mirror so you can watch," he ordered as he retrieved the ropes from the box.

She did as he requested, and he stood beside her. She expected him to tie her hands like he had at the club, but instead, he wrapped the longest piece of rope around her waist and fastened it by her navel, with equal lengths of the cord hanging on either side of the knot. And then quietly, and with purpose, he began weaving the ropes along her stomach and around her wrists, securing her arms to her sides, so tight that when she tried to move her hands away from her body, they didn't budge.

He glanced up at her face, a flicker of concern in his eyes. "Are you okay?"

She licked her bottom lip, surprised by how turned on she was by just this little bit of restriction. "You don't have to ask. I promise I'll tell you if it's too much."

He nodded, then continued entwining the ropes and using some of the smaller pieces to tie knots along pressure points in her lower back, her stomach, ribs, and sides. By the time he reached just below her breasts, her entire torso and arms were covered in purple stripes from the twine, and half a dozen intricate diamond-shaped patterns crisscrossed over her abdomen that actually looked...*beautiful* against her skin.

The rope and knots bit into her flesh, heightening her awareness, the light pinch of pain making her light-headed and shockingly aroused. She swayed on her feet and caught herself.

Sawyer tipped her chin up and stared into her eyes. "You still with me, sweetheart?" he asked gently, a small, amused smile on his lips.

"Mmmm," was all she could manage, but it seemed to satisfy him because he let his hand fall away from her face and grabbed the two hanging ropes beneath her breasts.

With concentration and precise movements, he wrapped each one around a mound of flesh and secured more knots, then tied off smaller pieces of rope and layered them over the fullest part of her breasts. The twine scratched across her sensitive nipples, and she couldn't hold back the moan that bubbled up from her throat or the rush of liquid warmth that spilled between her thighs.

He interlaced two more ropes to those and crossed them over her chest and over her shoulders. Through hooded eyes, she watched him work. Watched *him*. His breathing was deep and even, his expression etched with purpose, but there was no mistaking the authority in his touch, the dominant edge to his movements, or the massive bulge straining against the zipper of his jeans.

He gave the ropes between her shoulder blades another tug, then slowly circled around to stand in front of her. She thought she'd feel like a trussed up animal, but the entire act had been a sensual experience, and she felt high with desire.

Tracing his fingers along the ropes and his handiwork, he met her gaze, his eyes glowing hot and bright with lust and that adrenaline rush he'd talked about. "You look *stunning*," he said, his voice a low rasp of sound. He followed the diamond-shaped patterns all the way down her torso, and when he reached the apex of her thighs, he glided his fingers through her drenched pussy.

That one touch made her dizzy and almost set her off, but he was careful to keep his strokes just light enough to keep her on that quivering precipice of need.

Those wicked fingers dragged along her sex and through the slick, swollen folds. "Next time, I'm going to layer the ropes right along this soft, wet flesh, and tie a knot *here*," he promised in a sexy murmur and strummed her aching clit with his finger.

She could barely breathe, and it had nothing to do with being bound. Her weak legs shook, threatening to buckle under the need for a firmer caress, the need to *come*.

"Yeah, you'd like that, wouldn't you?" he asked knowingly.

The only answer she could manage was a soft whimper.

He lifted his hand to his mouth and sucked her juices off his fingers. "You taste so fucking good."

She closed her eyes and swayed once more, feeling euphoric, drunk. *Rope drunk*, she thought a bit giddily. Then she was literally swept off her feet as he carried her to the bed. He set her down in the middle of the mattress so that she was lying flat on her back.

"Jesus, Paige," he rasped as he came around to the foot of the bed and took in the lines of rope across her body, the knots that he'd formed, the patterns he'd made, before his gaze met hers again. "I need you so damn bad."

She realized his hands were fisted at his sides, his big body nearly shaking. He was silently asking for permission to take her. His expression was tight, fierce, leaving no doubt that once he was inside her, it was going to be a long, hard, rough ride. And Lord help her, she wanted that, too.

The new bold and brazen woman in her bent her knees and spread her legs, making room for him in between. "I need you, too," she said, speaking the truth and giving him the consent he'd been waiting for.

With a harsh exhale—as if he'd been holding his breath that whole time—he nearly tore off his jeans in his haste to get inside of her. He donned a condom, moved between her thighs, and hooked the back of her knees over his arms to hold her legs wide apart as he lowered himself completely over her. With the thick head of his cock lined up perfectly with her entrance, he slammed full length into her—so deep he filled all those empty, hollow spaces inside her—tearing a startled gasp from her throat.

Like an unstoppable force of nature, he thrust hard and fast, his hips jack-hammering as he tunneled relentlessly into her again and again. Wild. Driven. Unstoppable. Beneath him, she couldn't move, could only accept everything he had to give while she grabbed handfuls of the comforter to keep her anchored in the storm.

He rubbed his upper body against the ropes,

abrading his own chest and stomach with the twine, undoubtedly scratching and marking his skin. Both his hands speared into her hair, yanking her head back as he lowered his lips to her throat, his hot, damp mouth and his hotter tongue tasting her skin. Finding that sensitive spot where her neck and shoulder joined, he bit down, marking her, and that spark of pleasure-pain raced all the way down to her sex.

Another downward grind against her clit and she shattered, moaning deliriously as her entire being splintered into a thousand little pieces she wasn't so sure she'd ever get back. Her internal muscles gripped him, and Sawyer tossed his head back, the tendons in his neck straining and his lower body jolting hard against hers, violently, desperately. She vaguely heard him chanting her name, over and over, as his own orgasm claimed him.

Paige finally realized what it took for Sawyer to lose control completely, and she was elated that *she* had done that to him.

He collapsed on top of her, and her heart squeezed tight in her chest when he whispered a deeply pro-found "thank you" in her ear—knowing the fact that she'd allowed him to bind her so intimately had in turn given him some of that inner peace and calm that he craved.

Chapter Thirteen

SAWYER HELD PAIGE close to his side as they lay on her bed a short time later after he'd released her from his ropes, gently stroking her silky hair. The lights were out, and she slept snuggled against his chest, her deep, even breaths caressing his skin. He never wanted to let her go. And especially not after what they'd just shared and what she'd just given him so selflessly. Her trust. Her body. Along with a piece of her soul, even if she didn't realize that yet.

He knew without a doubt she'd found pleasure being bound, but the ropes were mostly about him and his needs, and she was the first woman who seemed to understand that. He'd tied up other subs before, but never one he *loved*, and now he knew there was no comparison to what he felt when he was with Paige and she was restrained in his ropes, granting him full control of the scene, of her. The pleasure it gave him was extraordinary. Sublime. And left him with a peaceful feeling he hadn't felt in too damn long.

He didn't like to dwell on the darker memories from his time in the military, but they still lurked in the shadows of his mind, a subconscious thing, yet still there. Paige was the calming presence in his life that he'd been searching for. He'd known it the first time they'd dated, and tonight only confirmed what he'd already realized and accepted.

But he didn't want her to have any regrets, and he was going to make sure that when she woke up in the morning, she knew what tonight meant to him, what *she* meant to him. That he didn't take her gift of trust for granted. That he wanted and needed her in his life and he planned on doing whatever it took to make her feel secure with him.

And in time, and with care, he hoped her forgiveness would follow.

THE SOUND OF someone moving around in her kitchen woke Paige from a deep sleep. She started to sit up in a moment of alarm, until she remembered that Sawyer had stayed the night and was most likely the culprit. And if she remembered correctly, he liked a strong cup of coffee in the morning to start his day.

She stretched her arms over her head, groaning

softly as muscles throughout her body ached in protest. Good Lord, she'd never felt so sore, even after going to the gym, she thought with a goofy grin on her face. But then again, she'd never had ropes pulled so tight and straining across her midsection and arms, around her breasts, and over her shoulders. She'd never been taken so well or so thoroughly.

When Sawyer had finally released the bindings, the rush of pleasure she'd felt through her body was almost the equivalent of an orgasm as her circulation had tingled and come back to life. That in itself had felt soooo good, as had the way Sawyer had taken care of her afterward. He'd insisted on rubbing her chafed skin with lotion, which had pretty much lulled her to sleep. She couldn't help herself. It had been an exhausting day all around.

She glanced at the clock on the nightstand. It was eight thirty in the morning, and because it was a Sunday, her normal day off, she didn't feel that panic attack to rush to the shop, even though she had a ton of work waiting for her there. It was quiet on Sundays, and without other distractions of phone calls or clients stopping by or Summer asking her questions, Paige actually got a lot done. She'd have breakfast with Sawyer, then head into the store.

She got out of bed and walked into the bathroom. She brushed her teeth, and one look at her reflection in the mirror revealed a very disheveled version of herself, as well as a woman who'd been well and truly fucked. She had to admit that she looked good like that, her skin flushed, her eyes bright, a satisfied smile on her lips. *And, oh my God*, Sawyer had actually left a *hickey* on her neck where he'd bitten her! Thank goodness she didn't have to deal with customers today.

With a shake of her head, she turned on the water, and as soon as it was hot, she got into the shower and stepped under the spray. She'd just finished rinsing the shampoo from her hair when the glass door opened behind her and Sawyer—completely, gloriously naked—joined her in the fairly spacious stall.

"Hey," she said softly, feeling a little bit shy about last night, even though she'd enjoyed every single thing he'd done to her. But the one thing that had changed was the fact that she didn't feel the need to cross her arms over her breasts or shift her body so her hips didn't look so wide. If her extra curves truly weren't issues for Sawyer, then why should they be for her?

Judging by the slight pull between his brows, something was bothering him. "Are you okay?" he asked, his voice reflecting his pensive expression.

"I'm fine," she assured him, way too distracted by the way the water slid down his chest, his abs, and lower. She wanted to follow the trail with her tongue.

His gaze searched her face, looking for some kind of confirmation. "After last night, I just didn't want you to…"

Pull away. She could see the words in his eyes, the concern that he'd pushed her too far, too fast. "I'm good, Sawyer." She smiled as she poured her peach soap onto the shower pouf. "*Really* good," she added to ease any other doubts.

His relief was palpable, and with a grin, he grabbed the sponge from her and began lightly buffing her chest, then around her breasts, careful not to abrade her still-sensitive nipples. "It's a gorgeous day out already," he said, scrubbing a little lower, then sliding the soap down her stomach and oh-so-gently between her thighs. "Want to run off and spend the day at the beach with me?" he asked hopefully.

That honestly sounded delightful, a day without responsibilities or a half-made bridesmaid gown that needed to be finished hanging over her head. Ugh. She hated that she had to turn him down. "I really, really can't," she said as he motioned for her to turn around so he could scrub her back, but she didn't miss the disappointment in his eyes. "In fact, these next two weeks are going to be nothing short of insanity. I'll be at the shop every spare moment I have, probably late into the night. Next weekend is the wedding, and the weekend after that the bridal expo. I have so much to do—"

"I understand," he said, cutting her off, though his voice wasn't at all gruff.

He dragged the pouf across her shoulders, down her back to her thighs, and into all the crevices in between. The man was incredibly thorough in everything he did.

She rinsed off, then turned back around so she was facing him. Before she could say anything or apologize, he spoke.

"After the wedding, and after the bridal thingy you have to do, do you think we could find the time to go out on a *real* date?" he asked as he hung the sponge back on its hook. "You know, dinner at a restaurant, a movie, coming back to your place and making out like horny teenagers on the couch like we did last Saturday at my place?" His tone was playful, but the heat in his eyes made her breathless.

She wondered if she'd ever get use to his effect on her. "Oh, I think we've gone way past that last part," she said with a laugh. "In fact, it's going to be incredibly hard to top last night."

He looked extremely pleased at her compliment, as well as the fact that she really was okay with that darker side to his personality.

He placed a hand on her chest and pushed her

back as he took a step toward her, until her shoulders were flat against the cool glass enclosure. "Well, if I can't spend the day with you, then I just need to get my fill of you now."

Her pulse leapt at his sexy insinuation, and liquid heat pooled in her belly. Just like that, she was aroused and excited. Wet in a way that had nothing to do with a shower. How was that possible when he'd utterly exhausted her the evening before?

She wondered if he felt the same. "You didn't have enough last night?"

"*Never* enough of you, Paige," he said huskily. "And I'm suddenly very, very hungry. Ravenous, actually, and I have a huge appetite in the mornings."

With a deviously wicked grin, he knelt in front of her, draped a leg over his shoulder to part her thighs to what he craved, and pressed his hot, open mouth to her pussy.

She gasped as his tongue slid between her folds, moaned when he added just the right amount of suction to that bundle of nerves that sprang to life the moment he captured it between his lips, and shuddered when he buried his face farther between her legs.

One of her hands reached out and twisted in his hair, and the other pressed flat against the glass cubicle for support as he speared his tongue deeper into her channel, then pushed two long fingers inside her sheath, fucking her with those digits as slowly and leisurely as his swirling tongue lapped at her flesh.

She made the mistake of looking down, of seeing the way she shamelessly rode his mouth, along with the wholly masculine expression on his face as he ate her, giving her so much pleasure that there was nothing she could do but surrender to his provocative ministrations. Her climax rolled through her body, tensing her muscles and flooding her limbs with sensation. She hissed between her teeth and let her head roll back until the orgasm ebbed.

He stood back up, looking extremely smug with himself, and completely drenched from the shower spray. He combed his fingers through his hair to get it off his face, then leaned more fully into her. He pushed his hard cock through her slick folds and groaned like a dying man.

"Fuck, I need a condom and I don't have any left with me."

Paige *really* wanted to reciprocate the pleasure and didn't want to resort to a hand job. She glanced over at the small, tiled bench in the shower cubicle and decided to fulfill a fantasy of his instead. Moving around him, she sat down on the edge of the wet tile and realized the height was perfect for what she had in mind.

She gave him her best come-hither smile. "Come here and I'll take care of that problem for you."

He raised a very interested brow, his gaze zeroing in on her mouth as he positioned himself closer, between her spread legs, blocking her from the shower spray. He clearly and eagerly expected her to suck him off, but instead, she filled her hands with her breasts and pressed them together.

"I want you to fuck my tits," she said, deliberately using the crude male version of the word, which made his cock twitch as if she'd stroked it.

His mouth fell open, then shut again as he stared at her with a combination of hope and disbelief. "Are you fucking serious?"

She rubbed her breasts together enticingly and even lightly pinched her nipples since she knew that drove him crazy, too. "Didn't you say you fantasized about it?"

"Yeah." He took his shaft in his hand, pumping it through his fist, making it harder, thicker than it already was.

Watching him stroke his cock was so incredibly hot, and she tried not to let the sight of his big, masculine hand wrapped around his erection distract her from what she'd intended. "Then do it," she urged him in a seductively husky voice. "I want you to."

He didn't hesitate a moment longer. Placing a hand

on the glass shower wall for balance, he fit the head of his cock between her breasts and gave a slow upward thrust of his hips. His shaft slid through that wet, slippery valley of flesh, the softness of her breasts surrounding him, cushioning him. The swollen crest peeked out the top, and Paige couldn't resist the urge to lower her head and lick across the sensitive tip.

"*Jesus*," he breathed, the muscles in his stomach flexing as he withdrew, then thrust back up again and again in a gradually increasing rhythm. He watched everything, his gaze turning a dark shade of brown and his expression fascinated and aroused.

A muscle in his cheek bunched, and it didn't take long for his breathing to turn choppy, erratic, and his eyes to glaze over with the beginning of an impending climax. She wet her bottom lip with her tongue and squeezed her breasts tighter together, massaging his cock and increasing the snug pressure around his shaft as his hips started pumping faster and faster, his chest heaving with every labored inhale and exhale.

Unexpectedly, he grabbed a fistful of her hair and pulled her head up as he bent over and his came down. His lips crashed against hers, and he moaned into her mouth as he kissed her deeply, greedily, their teeth clashing as he tried to consume her. And then he was grunting, his hips jerking hard, his entire body tensing as she felt the thick, hot surge of his release coating her chest, her breasts, as he came.

He shuddered a few more times, then finally released her lips so he could press his forehead to hers. "What a great way to start the day," he murmured in that sexy, satisfied voice of his.

She laughed and couldn't agree more.

SAWYER STROLLED INTO the offices of Noble and Associates after a day of security detail for a local client and greeted the receptionist with a smile. "Hi, Gail. I have a meeting with Mac," he said of one of the partners of the security firm.

The other woman nodded and returned his smile, even as she continued typing something into her computer. "He said to send you back to his office when you arrive. He's waiting for you."

"Thanks." He headed in that direction. The back area was quiet and deserted, but then again, it was nearly five o'clock in the afternoon on a Wednesday. When he reached Mac's office, he rapped on the open door to announce his presence and kept walking inside. Since Sawyer knew he was there to learn the specifics of an upcoming assignment that had just been arranged, which took a good fifteen minutes to a half hour of time, he sat down without waiting for the other man to offer him a seat.

"Thanks for stopping by, Sawyer," Mac said as he finished writing something down on a notepad and set his pen aside. "Earlier today I got a call from a client specifically asking to hire you for an evening of protection and security."

"Okay," Sawyer said, thinking it had to be a repeat client. "Who, what, when, and where?"

The corner of Mac's mouth tipped up in a grin. "The *who* is Melissa Moore. It's for security at a wedding reception this Saturday at her estate home in Fallbrook." Mac's gaze turned curious. "Do you know her?"

Sawyer hadn't yet gotten past the *Melissa Moore* part of the conversation. Paige's stepmother had called and requested *his* security and protection services for her wedding reception? Why *him*? Especially considering his past with both Ashley and Paige. Talk about an awkward situation, especially in such a personal, intimate setting.

"Yes, I know her," he replied hesitantly while trying to get a better feel for how he'd gotten roped into the job. "Did she say *why* she wanted me?"

"Didn't ask, and it doesn't matter," Mac said with a shrug as he leaned back in his chair. "Since the guy she's marrying is a solid client of ours, I'd like to keep him and, by extension, his future wife happy. Do you have a problem with the assignment?"

Sawyer bit his tongue. "No, sir," he replied. What was he going to say to Mac, anyway? That he didn't want to do the detail because he'd slept with his current girlfriend's stepsister? Yeah, that would go over well with his employer. Jesus, what a fucked up predicament.

"Okay, good." Mac nodded succinctly. "Jase will be doing the security detail with you."

Sawyer felt a small semblance of relief that his friend and co-worker would be there, as well. "So, just the two of us?"

"Yep." Mac shuffled through the papers on his desk, then handed Sawyer one of them. "Here's the time, place, and address. Your protection services are only needed until the bride and groom leave the reception, then you're free to go, as well. Oh, and she requested that you wear a tuxedo, since it's a formal affair. She wants the two of you to blend in and not look like security agents."

"Okay." Sawyer stood, the whole thing still sitting uneasily with him.

He headed out of the offices and down to his car. He had to let Paige know what was going on, and he had no idea how she'd react. Regardless, he'd have to suck it up for a few hours Saturday night, do the job he was hired for, and stay far, far away from Ashley.

✧   ✧   ✧

SAWYER WALKED INTO Couture Corsets with dinner for Paige, along with her favorite cupcake—red velvet—in hopes that the offering would soften the blow of finding out that he was going to be at a wedding reception that he had absolutely no desire to attend.

"She's in the back," Summer said when she saw him and grinned when she caught sight of the bags he carried. "And it's a good thing you brought food. Paige skipped lunch, and she's a bit snappy because of it."

He chuckled, not at all concerned about Paige's mood. "I can handle it and her," he said with a playful wink at the girl, then continued to the back of the shop and through the crystal curtain separating the front end from the work area.

Head bowed over a dress she was meticulously sewing beads and crystals on to, and her brow furrowed in concentration, she put a hand up as soon as she heard the curtain rattle. "I don't want to hear it. I can't deal with one more thing right now."

"You can't deal with dinner?" he said and set the two bags down on her worktable.

Her head whipped up in surprise, her green eyes wide. "Sawyer! I thought it was Summer coming back here."

She'd been so immersed in her project she obviously hadn't heard his voice out front.

He hadn't seen her since Sunday, and he drank in the sight of her. Her wild auburn curls were piled on her head in a messy knot, and her blouse was wrinkled and half untucked from her jeans. The slight shadows beneath her eyes accentuated how tired she looked, and yeah, she was a little grumpy judging by her initial greeting—but still so beautiful. He had the urge to take her home, draw her a bath, feed her, then put her to bed with him beside her and force her to rest.

"What are you doing here? Besides bringing me dinner," she said as she stuck her needle and thread into a small cushion that was strapped to her wrist and filled with an array of other pins. She nearly pounced on the bag containing the grilled chicken sandwich he'd ordered for her. "God, I'm *starved*."

For the moment, he evaded her first question and focused on her well-being instead. "You need to stop skipping meals. Why don't you just call a place that delivers?"

"No time, or I just forget about eating because I'm so freakin' busy right now." She unwrapped the sandwich, took a bite, and moaned appreciatively. "Thank you for this. It tastes so good," she said with her mouth full.

"The last thing you want to do is run yourself down," he said, resting his hip against the worktable.

"Not eating, working without breaks, not getting home until after ten at night, and up and out the door by seven."

"I'm fine. Or I will be once I finish this stupid dress." She glared at the gown she found so offensive.

Sawyer glanced at the froth of soft rose fabric and the top portion where she'd been adding the embellishments. "Is this the bridesmaid dress?" he guessed.

She nodded and swallowed another bite of her dinner. "Yes. It ended up being more work than I'd anticipated, but I need to get it done. The wedding is in three days."

He could see the stress of that deadline creasing her forehead and resisted the impulse to reach out and smooth his thumb across those tense lines until she relaxed. "The dress looks great to me."

She rolled her eyes at him. "You don't have the first idea of what goes into making a dress or any other garment, for that matter. Perfectly aligned seams and hems and making sure the chiffon fabric drapes down the front like it should without any puckers…"

She went on with the sewing speak, and even though it was the equivalent of her talking in Greek to him, he let her get it all out of her system. She was right, he was clueless about what kind of workmanship went into her designs, but he understood Paige well enough to know that she'd be meticulous and conscientious about her work, which showed in all the beautiful corsets that were on mannequins lined up against the wall. A lot of them were all white lace, satin, and brocade, but there were a few others in soft, muted fabrics of pink, lavender, and pale peach.

When she was done giving him a rundown of her sewing process and she'd finished off her sandwich, he nodded his head toward the lingerie. "What about all those corsets? Are they for clients?"

"No, those are for the bridal runway show," she said as she tossed her sandwich wrapper and bag into the trash. "I still have finishing touches to do on them, like accessorizing, making sure they fit all the models perfectly." She exhaled a deep breath, a glimmer of uncertainty in her gaze. "I have so much riding on this show."

"I'm sure it will be phenomenal," he assured her and pushed the second bag toward her. "I'm really proud of you."

"For?" she asked guilelessly.

"For all this," he said, waving a hand to encompass the entire boutique. "It's not easy running your own business, but you've really made something of your corsets and designs."

"I'm trying." She opened the small bag and peered inside, then glanced up at him with a smile that lit up her whole face. "You are such a bad influence on me.

All those treats from Extraordinary Desserts, and now this," she said, pulling out the clear plastic container with the cupcake inside.

He shrugged. "I figure you might need a little sugar rush to get you through the evening."

"Oh, definitely." She didn't hesitate to pop open the lid and use the plastic fork to take a bite, her eyes glazing over with pleasure as she savored the chocolate cake and cream cheese frosting. "Okay, now that you've plied me with food, what is the *real* reason you stopped by?"

Oh, yeah, *that*. "I wanted to tell you about a security job I was assigned today."

"Oh?" She raised her brows in genuine interest. "Something exciting?"

He laughed, but the sound lacked real humor. *It depends on your definition of exciting.* "Melissa called Noble and Associates to hire security for the wedding reception this weekend, and she asked specifically for me as one of the agents."

Paige stopped chewing and gave him a bewildered look. "Why would Melissa ask for you?"

"I wondered the same thing." He shoved his hands into the front pockets of his pants. "My gut is telling me that Ashley had something to do with it."

She nodded slowly, her complexion losing a bit of that rosy glow from moments before. "You're probably right."

He watched her push her half-eaten cake aside. His own stomach twisted in knots, as well, and he sought to reassure her. "I'd say no to the job if I could. And I realize this might create an awkward situation with me at the reception, but I'm there to do a job, nothing more."

"I know," she said and gave him a smile he knew was forced. "And I wouldn't expect you to turn down a job just because it's not convenient or it's uncomfortable for me." She shifted on her feet and lifted her gaze to his. "Besides, I trust you."

Sawyer lost his breath for a moment, because those words meant more to him than she'd probably ever realize, and she'd just given him a gift he wouldn't take for granted.

"Thank you," he said and hoped he was one step closer to a future with her.

Chapter Fourteen

S AWYER HADN'T BEEN back to the huge estate home where Paige had once lived since *the morning after*, as he was beginning to think of that day. Despite how uneasy he felt about being there, everything looked the same—elegant, refined, and expensive. Even the enormous backyard and courtyard had been transformed into a wedding wonderland, with twinkling lights everywhere and tables set up with fine china, crystal, and linens. Pale pink roses adorned *everything* and must have cost a small fortune, along with the towering centerpieces on every table that were overflowing with more exotic flowers and shimmering crystals. It was obvious that there had been no expense spared for the lavish affair.

"They're on their way in," Jase, Sawyer's buddy and co-worker, said into the microphone earpiece they each wore to keep in contact throughout the night.

"Time to take our places."

Sawyer gave Jase a nod as he positioned himself at the back of the event, hands clasped in front of him, while his co-worker stood at the other end of the yard. The five-piece orchestra started playing music as the guests who'd been at the church wedding arrived, filtering into the courtyard—the men dressed in tuxedos and the women in long formal gowns and glittering jewelry. Mac had told Sawyer that a lot of high-profile people would be attending the reception, and judging by the way they were dressed and the way they carried themselves, they were definitely wealthy and upper-class.

Sawyer caught sight of Paige's friend Kendall, who'd attended the nuptials as Paige's date. She strolled over to him, giving him a playful once-over, which was far better than the last time she'd greeted him with a glare and a threat at Paige's shop. She was wearing a black gown that was cut low in the front, and her dark hair was pinned back with a clip encrusted with crystals. Paige had told him that Kendall was thirty-five, but her friend looked as young and fresh as Paige's twenty-seven years.

"You look quite debonair in your tuxedo," she said in a deliberately hoity-toity voice. "Like James Bond."

He smirked but kept his gaze on the mingling guests and the white-gloved waitstaff, who were carrying around flutes of champagne and little appetizers for everyone to enjoy. "Where's Paige?" He was dying to see her, even if he couldn't *be* with her tonight.

"She's with the 'bridal' party,'" Kendall said while making air quotes. "The bride, groom, and Ashley. They'll be making an entrance soon. Melissa wanted them to walk in all together, like a family."

"Any drama between her and Ashley?" he asked curiously, since Kendall was well aware of Ashley's tendency to stir up trouble when Paige was around, and he knew she'd accompanied Paige to the pre-wedding preparations at the church.

"Just her normal little spoiled fits and rude comments," Kendall said drolly as she accepted a glass of champagne from a passing waiter. "Though I definitely saw a glimpse of a green-eyed monster."

He cast a quick, concerned glance at Kendall. "What do you mean?"

"Have you seen the bridesmaid dress Paige made?" she asked, then added, "Actually *on* her?"

"No." He'd only gotten a glimpse of the pile of fabric on her worktable and had no idea how the finished product had turned out.

"Well, she looks *stunning*. Absolutely *to die for*." Kendall's voice was infused with pride for her friend. "More so than Ashley, and everyone has been complimenting Paige on her dress, asking what designer created it and where she bought it." The other woman's eyes flashed deviously. "I think Ashley's plan to humiliate Paige in that tight-fitting dress backfired on her, and she knows it. And since Ashley doesn't hide her ugly feelings, it's clear she's jealous of the attention and envious of the dress."

Now that didn't surprise Sawyer at all.

"But of course Paige is a class act and has been downplaying the design of the gown," Kendall went on. "But it doesn't matter. I saw the resentful way Ashley was watching her. Paybacks and Karma are a bitch." She grinned and took a drink of her champagne.

Sawyer didn't care for the way that sounded. Resentment with Ashley would undoubtedly breed hostility, and that was the last thing he wanted Paige to have to deal with tonight. Then again, he could always hope that Ashley actually behaved herself on her mother's wedding day.

"So, who's your accomplice across the way who's trying to look inconspicuous but is clearly security for the evening?" Kendall asked, nodding toward Jase.

"That's Jase Burns. He works for Noble and Associates, as well."

"Hmmm." The sound Kendall made was definite interest. "Is he single?"

"*Yes*," Jase said emphatically into Sawyer's ear-piece, obviously eavesdropping on the conversation.

"As far as I know," Sawyer replied, shooting his friend an amused look. "You want an introduction after the reception?"

"Hell yeah," came Jase's eager reply. "Damn, she's hot."

"No, I can introduce myself," Kendall said with a shake of her head, oblivious to the voice yammering in Sawyer's ear. "Do you think he'd be interested in posing for some photos for romance novels?"

"*What the fuck*, man?" Jase said, his tone aghast.

It took effort for Sawyer not to burst out laughing, and he decided to have a bit of fun at his friend's expense. "I don't know if he would, but he does have that Ken doll look going for him."

"*G.I. Joe*," Jase countered, referring to the bad-ass hero action figure over the metrosexual doll with the perfectly coiffed hair and high-fashion wardrobe. "There is nothing *Ken-like* about this body, and my package is *way* bigger than his."

Sawyer snorted, which earned him a curious look from Kendall. He cleared his throat and averted his gaze back out to the guests. "Is that what you're doing now?" he asked the woman beside him. "Taking photos for book covers?"

"An author I know asked me to do it for her, and I

thought it might be a good addition to my photography business." She finished off her champagne and set the glass on a passing tray. "Boudoir is my main focus, but it never hurts to diversify. I'll have to see if your friend is interested in posing for me."

Jase groaned. "*Posing* is not what I had in mind."

The orchestra stopped playing, and a man tapped on a microphone to get everyone's attention. A hush fell over the crowd as he spoke. "The bride and groom are here. I'd like everyone to welcome Mr. and Mrs. Darren Burton!"

Everyone clapped, and Kendall glanced up at Sawyer. "I'd better go and find my seat," she said and quickly headed toward the tables, just as Melissa and her new husband walked into the courtyard with huge, happy smiles, followed by Ashley, who stood by her mother, then Paige, who stopped beside Ashley...as a family.

Sawyer stared at Paige, his mouth going as dry as dust as he drank in the sight of her. Kendall hadn't exaggerated when she'd claimed that Paige looked stunning and to die for. Actually, in his estimation, she looked like a gorgeous, exquisite goddess in the strapless gown she wore, with a crystal and beaded top—all hand sewn by her—and soft, flowing material that fell from her waist and swirled around her legs in delicate layers of sheer pink fabric. Both of the girls' dresses were the same color and fabric, but while Ashley's dress was tight and conforming and left little to the imagination, Paige's gown was beautifully constructed to subtly enhance her curves and easily trounced her stepsister's dress, even if that hadn't been Paige's intent.

She'd swept her hair away from her face and up into a fancy twist of some sort at the back of her head, and while Sawyer preferred her hair down, he had to admit the style was perfect for the strapless gown and showcased her sparkling green eyes and full pink lips.

Paige glanced around, and when she saw him standing in the back and away from the activity, she gave him a smile so sweet he had to resist the strong urge to take her in his arms and make sure everyone at the venue knew she belonged to him. Even if *she* wasn't ready to admit it yet.

The newly married couple, along with Paige and Ashley, made their way to the family table at the front. After a few speeches and toasts, the reception went into full swing, starting with a five-course sit-down dinner, followed by the dance floor opening up for those who wanted to cut loose.

Sawyer watched as Darren and Melissa went from table to table to greet friends, and he had to admit that the couple looked genuinely happy, even if Melissa had married him to support her lavish lifestyle. Or maybe they really were in love, and the guy's money was just a bonus. Who knew? It didn't matter to Sawyer. The only person he cared about in all this was Paige.

While watching the guests, he also kept an eye on Ashley, who was never far from Paige, despite Paige trying to keep her distance from her stepsister. Paige spent most of her time chatting with Kendall, but that didn't stop Ashley from glaring daggers at Paige every time someone complimented her gown or gave her more attention than Ashley was receiving.

A few hours passed, and the excitement gradually died down. Some of the guests started to leave, and as Melissa walked with some friends out to the front of the house to see them out, Sawyer turned his head to find Ashley strolling toward him, a glass of wine in her hand—her second one of the evening because he'd been counting. Everything inside of him tensed, especially when he realized Paige was watching her stepsister advance from across the courtyard.

Shit. Sawyer knew nothing good would come of Ashley interacting with him, but he wasn't surprised that she'd finally decided to approach him.

"I've got trouble heading my way," he said to Jase through the microphone. "Cover me for a few minutes."

"Isn't that Paige's stepsister?" he asked, obviously watching Ashley make her way toward Sawyer.

"Yeah, and she's my worst nightmare," he muttered. Jase had no idea what had happened between him and Paige's stepsister, so he knew his friend was going to learn real soon, depending on what Ashley said or did.

She stopped in front of him, blocking his view of Paige. "Having fun tonight?" she asked in a flirty voice that made his stomach churn because it was so damn fake.

There were a few people milling around, and while he would have flat-out ignored Ashley if they were alone, he knew he couldn't be rude with guests watching, considering he was the hired help. "I'm not here for fun," he said, his tone flat. "I'm working."

"And who do you think *got* you the job?" she asked, making it clear it was all her doing.

His jaw clenched so tight he was surprised he didn't crack a molar. "I didn't *ask* for the job."

"No, I just told my mother you were the best and that she needed to hire you for tonight, and here you are." She took a small sip of her wine and leaned in closer. "I thought it would give you the chance to finally realize what you walked away from that morning after you slept with me."

Her? Was she serious? The only thing he'd lost that mattered to him was Paige.

"The sex was amazing, by the way," she said in a

seductive tone as she touched a finger just below his bow tie and skimmed it down his chest. "You certainly know your way around a woman's body."

He grabbed her wrist and yanked her hand away, then immediately dropped it. "I don't remember a thing, Ashley," he snapped, tired of this game she was playing. "In fact, after drinking the beer *you* gave to me, I completely blacked out. I wonder how *that* happened."

She gave a shrug that neither confirmed nor denied what he'd insinuated. "Well, that didn't stop you from getting it up. You were all over me, and since you can't recall anything, I'll just let you know that you couldn't get enough."

Bile filled his mouth, and it took everything inside of him not to lose his temper as one of the guests walked by.

She tipped her head to the side, and he didn't miss the sudden vicious gleam in her eyes. "Tell me, aren't you getting tired of Paige yet?"

God, he just didn't understand how someone so pretty on the outside could be so ugly on the inside. "What the hell do you have against Paige?"

She rolled her eyes in disgust. "I just don't get what you see in her. She has no personality, she's a fat cow—"

"*Stop*," he said in a low voice that vibrated with

fury.

"Or what?" she pushed, sneering at him, *knowing* there was absolutely nothing he could do to her.

A person abruptly stepped between the two of them—Paige, he realized—and she pushed Ashley away with a shove that caused her stepsister to stumble back in her heels, but she managed to catch her balance, as well as keep her glass of wine from spilling.

"Back off, Ashley, or I'll rip all that pretty blonde hair right out of your scalp."

PAIGE'S HEART RACED a mile a minute as she stared down Ashley, something she'd never done before. Minutes ago, she'd watched Ashley approach Sawyer, had known by his body language that she was goading him, and refused to allow her stepsister to harass him any longer. She arrived just in time to hear her stepsister's hateful words, then Sawyer defending Paige. Yet Ashley had kept provoking him, and Paige had just had enough.

But now, they were at a stalemate, neither one of them backing down. Paige could feel the warmth and strength of Sawyer's presence behind her, but in front of her, Ashley's gaze was as cold as ice. The corner of her stepsister's mouth curled bitterly, and she slowly tipped her glass over and poured the red wine down the front of the dress Paige had spent so many hours working on.

Paige gasped in shock, devastated that Ashley had deliberately ruined her gown. Her heart twisted inside her chest at the knowledge that her stepsister's cruelty knew no bounds.

"*Ooops*," Ashley said malevolently.

"*Shit*," Sawyer muttered behind her and put a supporting hand on her bare shoulder.

Ashley narrowed her gaze, and Paige refused to look away, needing to hold her own with her truly evil stepsister.

Paige knew they were making a scene, that more and more people were looking their way, and she so did not want this confrontation between her and Ashley to be the highlight of Melissa's wedding day. "Just go, Ashley," Paige said, trying to keep her voice calm when her insides were a churning mess. "This isn't the time or place."

Ashley laughed, the sound harsh and mean. "God, you're so pathetic, Paige. Do you really think Sawyer's going to stick around? Zach certainly didn't. Once he got what he wanted, he was done with you, and Sawyer will be, too."

"Ashley!"

Melissa's horrified voice pierced the air, startling both Paige and Ashley. Her stepsister's head jerked around, her eyes wide as she realized that her mother had overheard her cruel words.

"What is *wrong* with you?" Melissa demanded, staring at her daughter with painful realization and sad acceptance of reality in her eyes. "And *why* would you pour your wine on Paige's beautiful dress or say those awful things to her?"

Ashley lifted her chin, showing no remorse. "Because they're true."

Melissa looked genuinely shocked and devastated. "Both of you girls, in the house," she said in a tone that brooked no argument.

Paige didn't hesitate. With a quick, apologetic look at Sawyer, she started for the back entrance, but Ashley didn't budge.

"*Now*," Melissa reiterated and grabbed Ashley's arm, something Paige had never seen her do before, forcing her daughter to follow.

Behind them, she heard Darren apologize to his guests, assuring them that it was nothing more than a sibling squabble, and urged them to enjoy the rest of the evening.

The house was quiet inside, and as soon as Melissa had the three of them in Paige's father's old study, she shut the double doors and looked from Paige to Ashley, who had a nasty look on her face.

"You've gone too far, Ashley," Melissa finally said,

shocking Paige with her statement. "Not only did you embarrass your sister in front of all those guests, but what you said to her…did you *do* something to humiliate her with this Zach person?"

"He was just a guy in high school who dumped Paige," she said with a shrug. "It wasn't a big deal."

Melissa's gaze returned to Paige, and the sudden knowledge in her stepmother's eyes made Paige's throat go tight.

"Paige, what happened?" Melissa asked softly.

"Nothing." Paige's voice sounded quiet and hoarse. "It doesn't matter." Which had been her standard reply to Melissa when she and Ashley were younger and her stepmother had overheard or seen Ashley do something mean to her.

Paige never said anything, never *tattled*, because she knew it wouldn't make a difference with Ashley, and even at a young age, she didn't think that Melissa would believe her side of the story over her own daughter, who she doted on. So, Paige bottled everything up inside. Every cruel joke. Every mean remark. All the hurt and humiliation and emotional agony that came with Ashley's hateful behavior.

"It *does* matter," Melissa said, and then her eyes widened, as if her mind had traveled into the past and she'd just realized that it was never *nothing*. "Oh my God. What *else* has Ashley done that you haven't told me?"

"Why do you care about her?" Ashley whined, but Melissa ignored her.

"Paige?" Melissa pushed for an answer.

Paige shook her head. She wasn't going there. She wasn't going to dredge up things that were in the past that couldn't be changed. She tried to swallow past the lump in her throat and blinked back the threat of tears.

Melissa turned and stared at Ashley, who feigned a bored look, while her mother's face was etched with pain. "You're my daughter by blood, Ashley, but I've always loved Paige just as much. But I'm just realizing that I wasn't a good mother to either of you, because whatever is between the two of you, it never should have gone this far. I should have been more diligent when you were younger, more aware of your relationship as sisters. I thought your behavior toward Paige was something you'd outgrow."

Melissa shook her head, sadness in her eyes. "For years, I've made excuses for your conduct, Ashley. I've tried to make up for your real father walking out on us and for what you lost at a young age by being lenient and trying to make your life easy. I've given you *everything* I never had. You want for nothing, yet it's still not enough."

Paige listened to Melissa's words, realizing for the first time that her stepmother hadn't seen her daughter's behavior because she was trying to make up for something lacking in Ashley's life. And as a result, never disciplining Ashley or calling her out on mean behavior had created an uncaring, self-centered, spoiled woman. A woman who hated Paige.

"It's time for you to grow up, Ashley," Melissa said. "It's time for you to stop resenting Paige for things that can't be changed."

Clearly, Melissa had deeper knowledge of Ashley's emotions and psyche that Paige did not, though she wasn't excusing any of her daughter's attitude or behavior any longer.

"Ashley, you owe Paige an apology," Melissa said.

Ashley gaped at her mother as if she'd lost her mind. "Are you serious?"

"Yes, I am."

Ashley laughed caustically. "Not gonna happen. I have nothing to apologize for." With one last enraged look at Paige, she stormed from the study and slammed the door hard behind her, making both Melissa and Paige wince as the walls reverberated with her anger.

Melissa came toward Paige, looking so beautiful in her vintage wedding gown but so incredibly despondent, too, on a day that should have been filled with joy and new beginnings.

"I'm so sorry I didn't see this sooner," Melissa

said, her contrition shining in her eyes. "That I didn't realize Ashley was treating you so badly, and for so long. A lot of this is my fault, too."

Paige didn't say it was okay but nodded instead to acknowledge her apology. Melissa pulled her into a warm hug, the kind that Paige could still remember her own mother and father giving her. The kind that was filled with affection and love and security.

It had been a long time since Paige had felt sheltered and secure, and she luxuriated in the moment, knowing and believing that Melissa did love her.

Chapter Fifteen

S AWYER WAITED ANXIOUSLY for Paige to return to the reception. As soon as she walked out of the house and he saw her expression, filled with more pain than he'd ever seen on her face before, he knew he had to get her out of there. Even though Kendall had driven Paige to the wedding and reception, Sawyer insisted on taking her home. With Jase remaining behind, Darren had generously allowed Sawyer to leave an hour before his shift ended.

In the car, Paige gave him a quick summary of what had happened in the house with Melissa and Ashley, then she grew quiet on the rest of the ride home. While Sawyer wasn't surprised about Ashley's angry exit, he was extremely grateful that Melissa had come to realize how badly her daughter had hurt Paige, and for so many years. And Melissa didn't even know half of what Ashley was capable of, or even the fact that Ashley had drugged and slept with him as some kind of vendetta against Paige.

So many nasty things had obviously been said out on that terrace by Ashley, long-ago secrets spilled that made him wonder at the depth of Ashley's bitterness and hatred toward Paige. During that confrontation, he hadn't been able to see Paige's face because she'd been standing in front of him, but he'd felt her body shake when Ashley had thrown out the insult about someone named Zach. Clearly, whatever had happened with this guy had affected Paige greatly.

He got her up to her apartment and inside, and was grateful when she didn't ask him to go home, because he didn't think he could leave her alone tonight, not like this. She looked so desolate, so incredibly wiped out by all that had transpired, and he just wanted to take care of her. Love her. If she'd just let him.

In her bedroom, he unzipped her now ruined dress and helped her out of it, then made her sit down so he could take off her heels and stockings. She wanted a shower, and even though he knew she was fully capable of doing everything herself, he didn't want to leave her side. He turned on the water to heat it up while she took off her bra and panties, and once she was inside the shower, he went back into her bedroom, tugged off his bow tie, and removed his tuxedo jacket, then his dress shoes and socks.

He stripped out of his shirt and took off his belt but left his pants on. Tonight wasn't about getting naked and having sex. It was about caring for Paige's emotional needs, especially when she seemed so lost and alone.

As soon as he heard the water turn off, he returned to the bathroom with a clean pair of her panties and a sleep shirt he'd found in her drawer. He held open a big, fluffy towel to wrap around her as she stepped out of the glass enclosure. He dried her off and dressed her but left her hair pinned up because it was easier for now.

He pulled down the covers and settled onto Paige's bed and made room for her beside him, and she didn't hesitate to climb up onto the mattress and curl up to his side. Her head rested in the crook of his arm, and she wrapped an arm around his waist, as if he were her anchor in the storm that had just blown through her life. He wanted to be that for her. Always.

There was something Sawyer needed to ask Paige. Something he needed to know and understand. "Paige, what happened with Zach?" The guy who Ashley had insinuated had slept with Paige, then dumped her. But Sawyer had a feeling there was a whole lot more to the story.

Paige stiffened against his side. It was clearly an

unpleasant subject for her, and he waited patiently for her to answer, or not. If she didn't want to tell him, he'd respect her choice and just hope that she'd open up to him in the future, because he certainly wasn't going anywhere anytime soon.

"Zach was a guy who dated me my junior year of high school," she finally said quietly. "He was good-looking, popular, and I was naive enough to believe that he really liked me. After we went out a few times, he pressured me into sleeping with him. I was a virgin, he was persuasive, and I gave in."

Sawyer stroked his fingers along Paige's bare arm. His stomach churned, and he braced himself for the worst, because he knew there was more coming.

She rubbed her cheek against his chest, and he felt her swallow hard. "The next day at school, Zach wouldn't look at me or talk to me. He acted like I didn't even exist."

Her voice was flat, emotionless, even though Sawyer knew how painful that memory had to be.

"When I asked him what was wrong, he told me that he didn't like fat chicks, and the only reason he'd slept with me was because Ashley paid him to."

Fuck. Sawyer willed his body not to tense, but the rage inside of him felt like a pressurized volcano threatening to erupt. He could easily imagine her pain, her humiliation, her devastation.

But destroying Paige's self-esteem was what Ashley did best, and because she'd been doing it for so many years, she'd set the stage for Paige's ongoing insecurities—about herself, her body, her self-worth. Was it any wonder that Paige had trouble trusting a guy's motives when it came to liking her or dating her?

He didn't need to hear any more about Zach. Didn't *want* to hear any more. But there was something important he needed to tell Paige. He came up on his side so he could look down at her, so he could look into her eyes, which were much too somber and sad after everything that had happened tonight, so stripped of any joy. *Defeated*. Sawyer refused to let Ashley crush what he'd worked so hard to build these past few weeks with Paige.

"I love you," he said with conviction and watched her lips part in startled shock. "You don't need to say it back. That's not why I told you."

Her wide eyes stared up at him, and he hated that he couldn't read her expression. But it didn't matter what she was thinking; she just needed to listen and hear him.

"I needed to make sure that you know how I feel about you, so there's no question in your mind going forward," he said, his pulse racing wildly as he laid his heart and soul bare for her—the first woman who'd ever earned it. Deserved it. "I fell in love with you a year and a half ago that day you bought me my coffee and bagel, and never stopped. And loving you means that I won't ever deliberately hurt you, that I'll do everything in my power to protect you and keep you safe. I'll always be here for you, through the good and the bad."

Her eyes shimmered with tears, and her throat convulsed as she swallowed hard.

"You deserve to be happy," he said huskily as he skimmed his thumb along her smooth jaw. "You deserve so much, and I want to give it all to you."

She bit her bottom lip and managed to blink back the moisture pooling in her eyes. "Thank you," she said, her voice sounding heartbreakingly shattered. Broken.

And it broke something inside of him, too, because there was nothing he could do to take away her pain, and he didn't know what was going on in her head. She clearly wasn't in any state to process his words or say them back.

He tucked her against his side, knowing tonight had stripped her emotionally, and he hated that once again he'd be out of town until next weekend. His biggest fear was that she'd have too much time to think, to climb inside her head and question everything he'd just said and tried to accomplish this past week with her.

Didn't matter. He'd just put his feelings for her on the table, and now she'd have the space to sort all this out for herself. He'd have to trust and believe that she'd come to the correct conclusion, that what they had together, what he'd tried so hard to build between them, was real and true.

PAIGE WAS SO grateful that the next week was over-whelmingly busy and exhausting as she finalized everything for her debut runway show at the bridal expo. During the day, it was a nonstop whirlwind of putting the finishing touches on the corsets and planning for the upcoming show that had the potential of taking her business to the next level, and at night, she was so utterly exhausted she climbed into bed and literally passed out from mental, physical, and emo-tional fatigue.

Sawyer texted her a few times a day—usually just short messages that didn't require a response, for which Paige was grateful. While his words and promis-es from last Saturday night were always in her mind, it was difficult to process any of her emotions when she didn't even have time to breathe and wouldn't until after the bridal event. And she didn't even know if Sawyer was going to be there, since he hadn't said anything about it.

The day of the runway show arrived, and with less than an hour to go until the presentation began, Paige's stomach was a jumble of stressful, anxious knots as she finalized the corsets and accessories for each model, and made sure the hair and makeup team she'd hired gave each of the women the soft, romantic, sensual look Paige wanted.

Her girlfriends had arrived early to help in any way they could. Kendall was there with her camera, taking photos for Paige's website, while Raina, Jillian, and Summer assisted the models with tying up their corsets and slipping into shoes and accessories. Stephanie, whose business was designing fantasy bedrooms, had decorated a gorgeous, stunning fantasy runway that rivaled a Victoria's Secret TV special, minus the angel wings on the models.

"You've got a packed house out there already, Paige," Stephanie said excitedly as she walked backstage, a huge grin on her face. "Standing room only in the back, and all the VIPs are in their seats anxiously awaiting the first look at your stunning new bridal collection."

Paige's stomach did another nervous flip at the thought of all the high-profile merchants she hoped to impress who were in attendance, awaiting a glimpse of her high-end corset designs. The VIP invitations she'd sent out to local upscale bridal shop owners had also included an invitation to an after-party meet-and-greet that Raina had insisted on setting up for Paige—with champagne, petite desserts, and the press in attendance, as well. Paige was confident that by the end of the show, when she had to speak, she wouldn't be as frazzled and could actually promote her line intelligibly.

But first, she had to get through the show, and she sent up a little prayer that it went off without any glitches. She glanced at the watch strapped to her wrist. Thirty minutes until show time.

"Paige, I need to run out to my car and get a bigger memory card for my camera," Kendall said, keys in her hand. "I'll be back in ten minutes. I didn't want you to think I ditched you," she teased.

Paige smiled at her friend. "Wouldn't have even crossed my mind," she said honestly. Without question, she could always depend on these five wonderful women in her life to never let her down.

Kendall rushed out, and Paige did last-minute checks on the corsets on the models to make sure everything looked perfect on each one. She'd looked in on all the girls except Sarah, her one plus-size model slated to wear the show-stopper corset encrusted in Swarovski crystals, pearls, and delicate beading that had taken Paige months to make—the spectacular, grand finale haute couture corset meant to empower women of all sizes to embrace their curves.

Paige looked everywhere, but she couldn't find Sarah, though she'd seen her earlier when she'd arrived. Paige hurried to the racks that had been delivered with all today's runway outfits. As soon as she saw the most important piece of her collection hanging there in its clear plastic garment bag, untouched, her stomach lurched with nausea.

She couldn't, for the life of her, figure out where the other woman had gone. Just then, Kendall came rushing back in, visibly upset as she headed straight toward Paige.

"What's wrong?" Paige asked.

Kendall wrung her hands. "I just saw your model, Sarah, leave."

"*What?*" Paige had to have heard her friend wrong.

Kendall's lips pursed. "I was on my way out to the parking lot, and I saw her talking to your sister. I have no idea what was said, but I did see Ashley give Sarah something, and then Sarah went to her car and drove away."

Ashley was here? Melissa had told Paige she wouldn't make it today because she'd still be on her honeymoon with Darren, and Paige never thought that Ashley would be interested enough to show up. But that was *before* their confrontation last Saturday. Now? With Ashley seen talking to Sarah, the only reason

Paige could think of for Ashley's presence was that her sister intended to somehow sabotage her runway show.

Frustration, anger, and dread clashed inside of Paige. "What am I going to do now? That corset is my finale and what completes the collection. It's *the* piece that everyone's anticipating," she insisted.

Raina and Jillian, who'd been standing nearby, came to her side. When they asked what was wrong, Kendall quickly explained the situation.

"Can you have one of the other models wear it?" Jillian suggested.

Paige shook her head, her distress increasing. "There is no way those size-two models can fill out that couture corset, and it won't cinch up tight enough. It was designed for a woman with full breasts and curvaceous hips."

The MC of the runway show came backstage announcing, "Ten minutes until show time, ladies! You need to get lined up! As soon as I introduce the Couture Corset line, the first model will start down the runway. Paige, as the designer, you'll come out last to greet the crowd, along with one last walk-through with the models."

A fresh surge of panic sliced through Paige.

"I have an idea," Raina said quickly. "Paige, *you* need to wear that corset."

Paige stared at her friend as if she'd lost her mind. "I can't," she automatically blurted.

"Yes, you can," Jillian said, reinforcing Raina's suggestion and bolstering Paige's confidence at the same time. "You don't have a model to do it, and you know that corset fits you perfectly."

Yes, it did, since Paige had originally sized it for herself, then hired a model with her same measurements. But the thought of walking out in that piece of lingerie, in front of hundreds of people, made a wave of nausea sweep over her, and all her insecurities rose to the surface.

"What better way to show everyone out there that corsets are for all shapes and sizes than to wear it yourself?" Raina asked, adding to the argument. "Those brides sitting in the audience aren't all skinny runway models. Most of them are average-size women, and they deserve to see that they can embrace their curves and be sexy for their man."

Paige's throat grew tight as she looked at the friends who were rallying around her, supporting her, so confident in her ability to pull this off. And suddenly, Paige knew she had to do it, because she *refused* to let her sister win at whatever hateful game she was currently playing.

"I need your help getting into that corset," Paige said to Raina and Jillian. "And we need to do it super quick before the show starts."

Jillian grinned at her, and the three of them whisked her away to the dressing area, where they helped strip Paige out of her current outfit, then into the corset and other accessories. Raina called over the makeup artist and hair team, and they bustled around Paige for a few minutes. When they were done, her three friends let out a collective gasp of awe.

"Oh my God, Paige," Jillian said as she turned her toward one of the mirrors in the small room. "*Look* at you."

Paige blinked at her reflection, barely recognizing the woman staring back at her. The gorgeous couture corset accentuated her curves in the best possible way, the white silk brocade, along with all the crystal embellishments, gleaming against her creamy skin. There was a peek of white satin panties, and the pair of white lace-top stockings made her legs look smooth, slender, and long. She'd embellished a pair of four-inch heels in crystals and pearls to match the corset, the exquisite shoes sparkling like diamonds on her feet. Glittering jewelry pieces shone from her ears, her wrists, and a double strand of pearls wrapped around her neck.

She felt and looked like a naughty version of Cinderella.

The entire ensemble, combined with her auburn

hair styled into soft, shiny waves over her shoulders and down her back and dramatic makeup that emphasized her green eyes and glossy lips, was absolutely stunning on her.

From the front of the stage, Paige heard the MC announce her Couture Corset bridal line and knew the first model had started down the runway.

"Come on, let's get you in line," Raina said as they rushed out of the dressing area.

"You work it, girl," Kendall said, giving her a last-minute pep talk so Paige had no time to give into the fear and back out of this crazy idea.

"You got this, Paige!" Jillian added, then gave her a gentle push toward the runway. "And smile!"

With one last deep breath for courage, Paige lifted her head high, squared her shoulders, and walked out onto the fifteen-foot-long platform that seemed to stretch on forever. As soon as she came into view, the audience let out a collective gasp of surprise and astonishment that was heard above the music. The spotlights and abundance of flash photography blinded her to most of the crowd, but she was able to see the bridal vendors and VIPs sitting at the edge of the runway, who looked up at her with enthusiastic smiles and excitement in their eyes that bolstered her confidence.

Her fears and insecurities fled as she embraced the

moment. This was everything she'd been working so hard to achieve, and there was no denying the sense of satisfaction that filled her at knowing that this was *her* moment, and nobody, not even her stepsister, could take that away from her.

She stopped at the end of the runway and glanced down, almost frowning when she saw Raina's fiancé, Logan, sitting in the front row, with Jase beside him. One more seat over, and her gaze met Sawyer's, who was staring up at her with a combination of lust and pride in his dark gaze. He was here! *Of course he was here*, her mind chastised, because she hadn't been so sure.

Her heart leapt crazily, then pumped furiously in her chest as he gave her a grin so hot and sexy it was nearly illegal in a public place. He stood up, clapping hard, and the entire audience followed suit, whistling and cheering in a standing ovation. The rest of her models came out to join her on the runway, and the applause increased in volume.

The reception for her bridal collection was better than she'd anticipated, but it was the man in front of her that mattered the most. The amazing man who made her feel beautiful and wonderful and sexy. The incredible man who loved *her*.

After a few minutes, Paige and her models returned backstage, which quickly turned into a crazy scene jam-packed with people wanting to take pictures and congratulate her, along with the bridal shop owners already expressing interest in her collection. There were even a few women who came up to Paige to thank her for creating such gorgeous corsets for brides who loved their voluptuous curves.

It was overwhelming insanity, and when she saw Sawyer trying to make his way through the throng of people, she started forward, meeting him halfway, her heart filling with love. He caught her up in his arms, and right there in front of everyone, he kissed her—a quick, hot melding of lips that was filled with desire and so much more emotion.

"Thank you for coming to the show," she said once he lifted his head and set her back on her feet.

"There was no way I'd miss it," he said gruffly. "You were breathtaking out there. And so brave and confident and sexy. I am so damn proud of you."

She grinned at his words, feeling lighter than air, even though she felt pulled in a dozen different directions at the moment. "I need to change before the after party so I don't ruin this corset. How about I meet you there?"

He nodded, though she could tell he was reluctant to let her go. Paige understood, because she felt the same way. She had so much to say to him, but this venue wasn't the time or place, and she knew any kind of talk about *them* would have to wait until later.

Once he was gone, the backstage gradually cleared out so the models, and Paige, could change. Fifteen minutes later, she was dressed in black slacks and a purple off-the-shoulder blouse and walking into the private party that Raina had put together for her. Guests were already drinking champagne and enjoying the desserts, but all Paige could see was Sawyer. He was talking to the guy friends he'd brought with him to the show, along with her best girlfriends. He glanced up as if sensing her presence, met her gaze with a smile, then started toward her.

Halfway there, his eyes shifted to something behind her, and a startling dark look transformed his features. Unsure what had caused such an abrupt change, Paige glanced over her shoulder and saw that Ashley had just walked into the party, uninvited, though she acted as though she had every right to be there.

Paige noticed that her group of friends—who also knew that Ashley had tried, *unsuccessfully*, to sabotage her show—were watching her stepsister's approach with worried looks on their faces.

"I'll take care of her," she heard Sawyer say, his tone vibrating with anger.

Paige shook her head at Sawyer and touched a hand to his chest to stop him from following through on the threat. She was so tired of Ashley's shit, so tired of her trying to ruin her happiness at every turn. It was ending, here and now.

"No, *I'll* take care of her," she said, knowing it had to be done.

Turning around, Paige started toward Ashley, stopping the vindictive woman before she could make her way into the party and cause another embarrassing scene in front of her guests.

"You're not welcome here, Ashley," Paige said, trying to keep things civil. "This is a private party."

She just laughed, the sound as ugly as her personality. "Do you know how ridiculous you looked out there on the runway in that stupid corset?"

Paige knew better, and there was nothing that Ashley could say to bring her down. Not anymore. "I'm done with you, Ashley," she said, knowing she had no choice but to cut her out of her life.

A bitter sneer curled her lips. "You can't be done with me," Ashley said. "I'm your sister."

"No, you were *never* my sister," Paige said, not backing down for a second. "You were someone I had to live with because my father married your mother. A mean girl who thought it was fun to torment me and break me down so you could feel good about yourself. And now that my father is gone, I have no ties or obligations to you."

Ashley's hands fisted at her sides, and her gaze

flared with hostility. "You don't deserve any of this attention," she said bitterly. "And as for Sawyer, he'll leave you as soon as someone thinner and prettier comes along, and then you'll have *nothing.*"

Paige actually felt a moment of pity for Ashley, because thanks to what Melissa had said last weekend, Paige now understood that her stepsister's insecurities and anger were a result of her own father walking away from her and never choosing to be a part of her life. Ashley wanted Paige to be just as miserable as she was, and Paige refused to give her that power any longer.

"That's not my future, Ashley," Paige said steadily. No, Ashley would be the one always alone.

Ashley seemed to grow more furious with every second that passed. "You will always know that Sawyer cheated on you with *me*, and you'll always wonder if he'll do it again."

Paige felt so remarkably calm, despite the fact that Ashley was trying desperately to provoke her. "I don't care what happened in the past with you and Sawyer. I trust him, and there is nothing you can say or do that will ever change that," she said truthfully. "I need you to leave *now*, and if you come near me again, I'll have no choice but to have you served with a restraining order."

Ashley glared and opened her mouth to say something, but Sawyer's friend Jase was suddenly there, grabbing Ashley's arm in an unrelenting grip. "I'll be happy to escort her out of the building for you," he said with a bad-boy grin and guided Ashley back toward the door, giving her no choice but to follow.

When Ashley was gone, everything inside of Paige felt lighter, freer. Like a huge weight had been lifted off her chest. She turned back around, and Sawyer closed the distance between them, a worried look creasing his brow.

"Are you okay?" he asked gruffly.

Paige glanced just beyond Sawyer, seeing the people who were the most important in her life. The best girlfriends in the world, who built her up, were always there for her, and accepted her for who she was, inside and out. The kind who empowered one another, like *real* sisters should. And Sawyer, who made her feel beautiful, like she could do anything in this world as long as he was by his side. Sawyer, so patient. Sawyer, the man she loved without question and wanted to spend the rest of her life with.

This group was her family, and Sawyer, he was her future.

Paige's heart overflowed with emotion and an abundance of love as she looked back at Sawyer.

He wanted to know if she was okay. She smiled at him and answered, "Actually, I've never been better."

✧   ✧   ✧

IT WAS LATE afternoon by the time Paige was done for the day—with the runway show, the after party, and the cleanup, which Sawyer helped with, as well. As much as he was dying to be completely alone with her, he bided his time. Today was *her* day, and she deserved to enjoy every second of it.

Since Summer had driven Paige to the bridal expo, Sawyer was able to drive her home. As they walked into her apartment, she floated on air, her happiness and exhilaration tangible. She was high on success, and he absolutely loved the look on her. The flush on her face, the sparkle in her eyes, and the elated smile on her face were sexy as hell.

He set down the bags of runway stuff he'd carried upstairs for her, resisting the urge to sweep her off to the bedroom to celebrate with her in a whole different way. They hadn't had the time to talk, *really talk*, all afternoon. Once Jase had escorted Ashley out of the after party, Paige had been inundated with attention from all the VIPs. Wanting her to feel free to talk to everyone, he'd watched her work the room from the sidelines, so impressed with her business savvy and that dazzling personality that had new clients and high-end bridal designers eating out of the palm of her hand. There was no doubt in his mind that this was just the beginning of her business becoming a well-known brand name.

She dropped her purse onto the couch and exhaled a deep sigh that was filled with contentment and the last traces of excitement still coursing through her.

He walked toward her, grinning. "The life of a runway model is exhausting, isn't it?"

She laughed and shook her head. "That was my first and last runway show as a model, *ever*," she insisted, her eyes dancing playfully as she watched him close the distance between them.

"I know I already told you this, but you were spectacular on that stage." Reaching her, he slid an arm around her waist and brought her flush to his body. "Absolutely jaw-droppingly gorgeous and hot. I was so fucking proud of you, but I have to admit I wasn't thrilled that you were nearly naked in front of so many people." He feigned a frown.

"I wasn't even close to half-naked," she said with a roll of her eyes as she wrapped her arms around his neck. In the next moment, she grew serious, her gaze lifting to his. "What I did today on that runway, I couldn't have done it without you."

He gave her a curious look. "I had nothing to do with it."

"You had everything to do with me being confident enough to step out on that stage in a corset in front of so many people, without the fear of being judged or criticized." Her eyes filled with an emotion that grabbed at his heart. "Thank you for making me feel so beautiful, so desirable. And so secure about you and us together."

To hear her say that was huge and flooded him with relief. "What you said to Ashley, about not caring what happened between her and me in the past—"

"I meant every single word," she said, obviously sensing his need for reassurance. "I don't want to live in the past anymore, where Ashley had too much power to hurt me. Not anymore. I want to live in the present, with you, and never look back."

Damn, he adored this woman. He cupped her face in his hand and brushed his thumb along her cheekbone. "Thank you."

She shrugged. "I trust you," she said simply.

He swallowed hard and asked about the one thing he needed the most. "And you forgive me?"

"Better than that." She lifted up and pressed her soft lips to his and whispered, "I love you, Sawyer Burrows. *So* much."

Groaning at her sweet, perfect declaration, he kissed her, his tongue sliding into her mouth, his body pressing against hers, his hands tangling in her hair to hold her steady so he could drink his fill of her. As if he'd ever get enough. Not possible, he knew. Even forever would never be long enough.

He lifted his mouth from hers but still held her

close. "Do you know how badly I wanted to get you alone all day so I could have my wicked way with you?"

"You're alone with me now," she teased, her eyes filled with desire as she wriggled her hips against his, rubbing against his erection and something else he had in his front pocket. Her eyes widened a bit. "And you seem to be very, very happy about that. When did you grow an extra two inches?"

He chuckled. "Impressive, right?" he drawled, then let her go so he could reach into his pocket and pull out the black velvet box that he'd put there this morning, in hopes that the day would end just like this.

When she saw what was in his hand, she gasped, and her gaze shot back up to his. "Sawyer?"

He swallowed hard, even though everything about this moment felt so right. "Do you remember when I told you that I never stopped loving you?"

She nodded, eyes huge, but she remained mute.

"You've been a part of me for the past year and a half, even when I thought we might never have another chance together," he said, opening the box so she could see the diamond engagement ring inside. "Now, I'm never letting you go. Marry me, Paige. Be my wife. I want to build a family with you and make a life together. Forever. Say yes, and I swear I will make you the happiest—"

"Yes," she interrupted him with a delighted laugh. "Yes, I'll marry you."

He slipped the ring on her finger, and she looked at it in awe and complete delight.

"It's gorgeous," she breathed.

"What do you say we take this into the bedroom?" he asked and unexpectedly swept her into his arms, loving her squeak of surprise as he carried her in that direction. "We have a lot of celebrating to do."

Her eyes shimmered with excitement as she looped her arms around his neck. "Are we breaking out the ropes?"

He enjoyed the ropes and would no doubt tie her up again in the near future, but it was no longer something he felt compelled to do. Right now, at this moment, the only thing he wanted was Paige. "I think I'm in the mood for another show tonight," he said, giving her a heated look as he stopped by the bed and set her on her feet. "A show I've never seen before but have fantasized about a hundred different times. You, straddling my hips, completely naked except for that engagement ring on your finger, riding me hard while I watch."

She bit her bottom lip, her excitement undeniable. "I'm all about fulfilling fantasies, and I even have a few of my own I'd like to try," she confessed unabashedly.

"Then we'd better get started," he said with a grin that promised all kinds of decadent pleasures.

Now and forever.

If you enjoyed Paige and Sawyer's story, please consider leaving an honest review for
PLAYING WITH PLEASURE
at your e-tailer. It only takes a moment and is very helpful in spreading the word to other readers.
Thank you!

To stay up to date on Erika Wilde's latest releases, please sign-up for her newsletter here:
www.erikawilde.com/social-newsletter-sign-up

Next up, Kendall Shaw and Jase Burns in
PLAYING WITH SEDUCTION!

PLAYING WITH SEDUCTION

Kendall Shaw loves her job as a boudoir photographer. When she enlists hot, gorgeous, 100% alpha male, Jase Burns for a custom photo shoot for a romance novel cover, she quickly discovers that he only took the job to get close to her. But her painful divorce has made her wary of men, and especially one who is eight years younger than she is.

The moment Jase sets his sights on beautiful, sexy Kendall, he wants her. Despite their mutual attraction, she's rejected his every advance. But Jase loves a good challenge, and one steamy, seductive night at The Players Club changes everything between them.

Kendall has never experienced such overwhelming passion, or been pursued so tenaciously. Jase is addicting, in every way, and she soon finds herself falling for a man who doesn't fit into her ideal future.

Can Jase convince Kendall to let go of her past and take a risk on a second chance at love—with him?

Order PLAYING WITH SEDUCTION!

Other Books in The Players Club Series

Book 1: Playing with Temptation (Raina and Logan)
Book 2: Playing with Pleasure (Paige and Sawyer)
Book 3: Playing with Seduction (Kendall and Jase)

More Players Club Stories Coming Soon!

Other Books by Erika Wilde

The Marriage Diaries Series

THE AWAKENING (The Marriage Diaries, Volume 1)
THE SEDUCTION (The Marriage Diaries, Volume 2)
THE TAKING (The Marriage Diaries, Volume 3)
THE TEMPTATION (The Marriage Diaries, Volume 4)
THE INVITATION (The Marriage Diaries, Volume 5)
THE CAPTURE (The Marriage Diaries, Volume 6)

To learn more about The Marriage Diaries and interact with the series and characters, please like my Erika Wilde Author Facebook Fan Page at:
www.facebook.com/erikawildeauthor

About the Author

To learn more about Erika Wilde and her upcoming releases, you can visit her at the following places on the web:

Website:
www.erikawilde.com

Facebook:
www.facebook.com/erikawildeauthor

Twitter:
www.twitter.com/erikawilde1

Goodreads:
www.goodreads.com/erikawildeauthor

If you enjoyed PLAYING WITH PLEASURE, I highly recommend the newest book by Alannah Lynne. COVETED is hot and erotic, but extremely emotional, as well. I hope you enjoy the excerpt below!

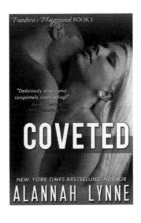

She's his heaven and his hell...

Muriel Stewart has spent the past year grieving the loss of her husband. Now that time has passed, her inner submissive demands Muriel find a new relationship to fulfill her need to love and serve. But there's only one man who makes Muriel yearn for the intimate Dom/submissive connection the way her husband did, and that's his best friend, Mathew Galinda ... a man who can barely tolerate her presence.

Matthew Galinda buried his own heart and needs the day Muriel Stewart married his best friend and business partner. He's spent the last eleven years keeping Muriel at a distance, tortured by his love for a woman he could never have, and filled with shame for coveting what wasn't and would never be his. Not even his best friend's unexpected death could change that fact. Until Muriel decides she's ready for a new Dom and wants Matthew to fill that role.

Having Muriel in his life is all Mathew has ever wanted. She's his heaven and his hell, and could be his salvation if he can get beyond his past, his shame, and the guilt he feels for not having saved Ian's life.

Chapter 1 of COVETED

A S HER CAR'S brake lights flashed on and off, then disappeared into the nearby parking garage, a spear of paralyzing fear shot down Muriel Stewart's spine and into her legs, anchoring her four-inch Jimmy Choos to the sidewalk like lag bolts.

With her only method of escape out of sight, she turned her gaze to the broad steps and heavy wooden doors in front of her, opened her mouth, and drew in a deep breath of cool evening air. She'd gotten used to flying solo over the last year, but the tightness in her chest and the lack of oxygen reaching her lungs proved there were still a few things she wasn't comfortable doing alone.

Visiting Pandora's Playground was apparently one of them.

"Oh, c'mon, Muriel," she growled through clenched teeth as she fisted her hands at her sides. "This is ridiculous."

Pandora's Playground had been a second home to her late husband, Ian, and her over the past three years—four if she counted the year they'd spent transforming the old live-performance theater into one of the most exclusive kink clubs in the southeast.

All their closest friends were members, and there wasn't any place she felt more comfortable, or loved, than at the club.

However, at the moment, she felt like a wild animal: frightened and cornered with no means of escape, even though she stood at the edge of a wide open street.

She brushed away a piece of hair tickling the corner of her eye and futilely wished the suffocating panic closing in on her could be so easily swept away. It wasn't supposed to be like this. She wasn't supposed to arrive alone at a club like this. She was supposed to be with Ian.

Dammit, why did I agree to come here tonight?

Because rather than using his concerned-friend voice to initiate the invitation, Master Lucas had spoken to her like a Dom commanding a sub. "Be at the club Friday night, eight sharp."

Before her brain cells established a defensive position and declined the invitation, her compliant, submissive soul stepped forward and spoke on her behalf. "Yes, Sir."

She could've called him back and told him she had plans she'd forgotten about and couldn't make it, but the truth was she missed Pandora's and her friends. She missed her old life… and her old self. Following his command, she'd arrived precisely at eight, but her resident scaredy-cat kept waving her paw, reminding Muriel that while he'd told her to be at the club at eight, he hadn't actually said anything about *entering* the building.

The overhead canopy loomed like an ominous dark cloud, but the embedded lights casting a glow over her no doubt illuminated every fear and worry line creasing her face.

She lifted her gaze to the security camera mounted in the corner and stared at it like she could see through the lens and into the eyes of the man she knew was watching.

If she continued to stand there looking desperate and pathetic, would he take pity on her and come to her rescue?

No, probably not. Lucas Steele was the most patient man, as well as one of the most disciplined Doms, she'd ever met. Even if it took her hours to make up her mind, he would patiently stand in front of the monitor, watching and protecting from a distance, just as he'd done for the past year.

The problem was even though she was physically safe and sound, she was an emotional mess. She huffed at the notion that would matter to him. He was a Dom... He thrived on keeping submissives in a state of upheaval. Her emotional earthquake sure as hell wouldn't spur him into action.

She chewed her bottom lip and returned her attention to the doors—the ones she'd never walked through alone. The prospect of doing so tonight threw a wash of sadness over her, burning her eyes and causing her to sway on the stilettos Ian loved so much. Without his warm, loving hands to steady her, she had no choice but to grab hold of the cold, brass handrail and support herself.

The sight of her bare ring finger intensified the burn in her eyes and forced her to clamp down on her lip to stop the trembling.

"You're not here to play, Muriel. You're here to visit with friends... and maybe... possibly... if it feels right... start slowly moving forward with your life."

Which meant she needed to start moving in the direction of those damned doors before she got ticketed for loitering. Having Lucas play witness to her chicken-skinned approach was bad enough. She didn't need the added embarrassment of the valet returning from the garage to find her rooted where he'd left her.

With a deep breath, she concentrated on the toes of her shoes as she lifted first one foot, then the other, slowly... cautiously... climbing the red-carpeted steps to the club's grand entrance.

The vertical brass handles were icy under her fingers and the heavy door seemed to pull against her as she tugged it open. The warm ambiance of the lobby reached out invitingly, so she slipped through the crack in the door and stepped inside.

The theater's original entryway had been a large, open space that allowed show-goers to congregate and visit before the performance. Ian, Lucas, and Mathew had reduced the size of the room to create a more intimate setting, as well as making more space in the interior of the club for playrooms. Even though they'd redistributed the space, they'd worked hard to preserve the original ambiance and had far exceeded everyone's expectations, including their own.

Heavy red velvet drapes hung on either side of the ticket window, which now functioned as the reception area and coat closet. Reproduction wallpaper lined the walls, and reflected the warm light cast by the original gas wall sconces. If one closed their eyes, they could almost hear the laughter and chatter of all those who'd filled the room decades before.

To the left of the coatroom was a modern office, which housed the monitors for the security cameras covering every inch of the club, including the sidewalk out front. She found Lucas exactly where she'd expected—leaning against the doorway of the office where he could keep an eye on the camera monitoring the sidewalk as well as the front door itself.

His tender smile and the pride shimmering in his green eyes warmed her heart and soothed the sharp, raw edges of her nerves. "You're such a brave girl."

She laughed and dropped her chin to her chest, hiding her embarrassment at having been caught flat-footed… well, as flat-footed as a girl could get in four-inch heels. "I don't feel very brave." She slid her toe through the thick-pile carpeting and twisted her mouth into a pout. "You could've come out and gotten me."

"I could have," he said, shoving off the doorway to close the distance between them to envelop her in a tight, welcoming hug.

His arms wrapped protectively around her, as well as the press of his solid body against hers, made her glad she found the guts to shuffle her butt through the door. As a massage therapist, she touched people on a daily basis. But no one ever touched her.

It'd been a year since anyone held her close, and until this moment, she hadn't realized how much she missed the physical connection.

When he relaxed his grip, she reluctantly followed his lead and stepped away from the warmth of his embrace. "You know why I didn't come for you, right?" His moss-green eyes roamed her face, searching for clues that she understood why he'd left her alone.

She sighed and nodded. "If you'd saved me, you wouldn't know if I'm ready to be here or not."

The corner of his mouth kicked into a lopsided grin and his eyebrow rose a fraction of an inch. "*I* know you're ready. Otherwise, I wouldn't have called you…" He let the sentence trail off, allowing her to assimilate the rest on her own.

She smiled, then dipped her head and drew in a deep breath. She knew the answer he was looking for, and she needed a minute to make sure she gave him complete honesty. Lifting her gaze to meet his, she drew her shoulders back and gave him the most reassuring smile she could muster. "I needed to know I'm ready." And after nearly a year of grieving the loss of Ian, she figured she was as ready as she would ever be.

"Brave and smart," he said, slipping an arm around her shoulder before dropping a kiss to the top of her head. "You'll do all right here."

Laughing along with him came easy until her gaze slid to the heavy wooden doors leading into the heart of the club. By sheer force of will she'd gotten inside the building, but standing in the lobby was easy. Now that she was close enough to hear the steady bass of the heart's beat, doubt crept back in on a wave of nervous energy. Her smile froze as her muscles contracted and a chill swept across the back of her neck and down her arms.

The club hostess, a young submissive, judging by the way she was dressed and kept her gaze lowered, had been quietly standing off to the side, smiling awkwardly and playing with the registration book on the counter. As if picking up on Muriel's tension and realizing something needed to be done to break her frozen limbs loose, she cleared her throat and said, "Master Lucas, as your guest, does she need to sign in?"

Lucas's carefree laughter filled the lobby and wrapped around Muriel, helping to ward off the chill that had grabbed hold of her and threatened to drag her out of the building. "She isn't a guest, Chrissie. Not only is Muriel a founding member of the club, but she's one of my business partners." His grin widened as he winked at the girl. "I guess, technically, that makes her your boss."

"What?" Muriel sputtered. The shock of his statement was enough to break her free of the frozen animation that had captured her, and she whipped her head around to face Lucas so fast she made herself dizzy.

He cocked his head to the side and gave her a blank stare. "Who"—a shadow crossed his face as his smile faltered—"who created Pandora's Playground?"

"You, Mathew, and Ian."

Three men from three very different walks of life who found each other in college and became closer than brothers with an unshakable bond.

Lucas nodded and swallowed hard. "Who owns Ian's shares now?"

She pressed her lips together and fought the knot filling her throat. In the year since Ian's passing, she'd left all the legal matters to Matthew, an attorney, because she knew he'd take care of things just as Ian had. They'd never talked specifics, and she'd never thought about what happened to Ian's share in Pandora's, but since all of his assets transferred to her…

"Well, hell." She gave the girl a *whatdya know* look. "I guess he's right. About being an owner, anyway. Forget all that being-a-boss business."

Chrissie flushed and dropped her gaze to the counter. "I'm sorry, ma'am. I didn't recognize you."

"Oh, sweetie." Muriel reached across the counter and squeezed her hand. "I'm not a Domme, and all this ownership stuff is on paper only. There's no need to ma'am me. There's also no way you would've recognized me." She released the girl's hand and cleared her throat. "I haven't been here in a long time."

Too long, a tiny voice whispered in her ear, while another part of her still questioned if she'd waited long enough.

She swallowed hard as her stomach pitched and rolled like an angry sea. Nervous and jittery, she turned to Lucas, the only lifeline she had at the moment. "Walking through those doors is bound to set off an avalanche of emotions. Even though I'm not playing, I'm not sure I'm ready for this."

As the words left her mouth, she settled her gaze on the floor so he didn't pick up on the twisting uncertainty in her eyes. The most important element in any relationship was honesty, and that includes one's relationship with themselves. If she were to play by the rules and be completely honest with herself right now, she might be forced to admit some of her emotional distress came from knowing she *wasn't* playing.

For the past year, a significant part of who she was as a woman had been locked away. The stifled submissive had been making a lot of noise lately, demanding more and more of Muriel's attention, but Muriel wondered if she'd ever be able to bring her out into the light again.

She'd never submitted to anyone but Ian. She hadn't even known she was a submissive until he unlocked the hidden door and coaxed her out of the dark into the world. She missed the exquisite bond forged between a Dominant and his submissive and had begun to wonder if she'd ever be complete without it. But the thought of moving on without him left her off balance and riddled with guilt.

As Lucas continued to study her, no doubt evaluating her body language and facial expressions to figure out where her head was at, the outer doors opened and a couple entered the lobby. She recognized the man as Kevin Mazze, the contractor who did the majority of the renovations on the building. Beside him stood a petite blond, who looked as nervous and conflicted as Muriel felt.

Lucas leaned in close to Kevin and spoke in a low voice intended for Kevin's ears only. Kevin responded in kind, then the two men laughed before Kevin took his lady friend's coat and handed it over to Chrissie. As the couple stepped up to the doors, Muriel gasped with shock at seeing wedding bands on their hands.

Wow... Wildman, who Ian believed would never settle down, is married.

As he looked down at his wife with an intimate, reassuring smile, her chest rose and fell with sharp breaths and she latched onto and held his gaze as if the connection with him was the only thing keeping her alive. He kissed her mouth, then moved on to the soft skin of her inner wrists. As he slipped on cuffs and buckled them in front, she whispered, "I love you," then dropped her gaze to the floor.

The love flowing between them was a living, breathing thing and was almost more than Muriel could bear. Her chest constricted and she nearly crumpled with grief for all she'd lost as well as a deep longing for the chance to share that kind of love again.

Watching the woman's transformation from a loving wife to a devoted submissive who would crawl across broken glass if it would please her Dom, touched Muriel on a cellular level. Her inner submissive cried out with need, and Muriel squeezed her eyes shut to stop the tears stinging the backs of her eyes from making an escape.

An ache in her hand drew her attention away from the couple and down to where she'd latched on to Lucas's forearm so tightly her knuckles were white. She snapped her gaze to his, not the least bit surprised to find him watching her intently… knowingly.

Music from the bar flooded the lobby as the couple opened the doors and disappeared inside, leaving Muriel alone with Lucas and his all-seeing eyes.

She released his arm and squeezed her eyes shut. She couldn't do this. She couldn't go in there…

But she also couldn't leave without at least giving it a try.

"I'm sorry," she said weakly as she brushed the wrinkles out of his sleeve. "I'm so confused. I know I need to get back into the game of life, but I don't know how."

He linked his fingers with hers and brought her

hand to his lips. "You take baby steps, and let us help you feel your way along. Being here is a good start." He stepped behind her and removed her coat, then handed it over to Chrissie. Returning to Muriel, he wrapped his arm around her shoulder and squeezed. "Everyone here loves you, and no one will allow any harm—physical or emotional—to come to you. You know that, right?"

"I know. I could never go anywhere else and do this."

"There's no need to go anywhere else." A wicked shimmer lit his eyes, causing a surge of panic to mix with excitement that created a massive dose of trepidation. But before she could put the brakes on her rubbery legs and stop the forward momentum, he opened the door, pulled her into the cavernous interior of Pandora's Playground, and said, "Everything you need is right here."

*　　*　　*

MATHEW GALINDO ALWAYS figured he was on the fast track to hell, and tonight's fun and games would certainly be an up-close and personal preview of the misery and suffering the fiery depths would bring. Nothing screamed *WELCOME TO HELL* louder than having everything he ever wanted laid in the palms of his hands... and rather than being able to hold the precious gift close to his heart to keep and cherish forever, he would have to force his fingers apart and let the promise of salvation sift through like dry sand.

Jesus.

He scrubbed his hands over his face and huffed with seething frustration. How would he ever get through the night with the little bit of humanity he'd managed to retain over the years still intact?

The beam of light from the lobby slashing across the bar's hardwood floor as the door opened, along with the gasp of surprise and the ripple of excitement that rolled through the crowd told him the guest of honor had arrived.

But he didn't needed to see, hear, or feel any of those things to know his personal Kryptonite had arrived. The burning in his chest from his seized lungs and the beads of sweat rolling down the back of his neck were warning enough.

Anytime Muriel got within fifty feet of him, his molecular makeup shifted and instantly realigned to her frequency. His body honed in on her like a guided missile and no matter where she was or how hard he tried to fight the pull, he stayed locked on her until she left the premises.

She hadn't taken more than ten steps into the club before the members swarmed her. Standing just inside the doors, the light from the EXIT sign cast an unholy red glow over her blond hair and pale dress—which was appropriate for how he viewed the evening, but the image was all wrong for her. She might be the tormentor of his soul and the reason his life was a living hell, but she was the closest thing to an angel he would ever see.

Her long, blond hair, brilliant blue eyes, and a dazzling smile caught the attention of anyone within sight of her. But her wide open heart and deeply compassionate nature gave her an ethereal glow that drew people in and kept them captivated.

From the stark contrast of their physical appearances—her blond hair to his black; her blue eyes to his brown—to the cool, emotionless void of his inner being, she was his opposite in every way.

The first time he laid eyes on her, her light pierced his cold, black heart and he'd instantly recognized her as his mate.

The problem was she'd been on his best friend's arm, laughing at his witty charm and looking at him with adoring eyes, completely oblivious that Mathew was even in the room. Ian had brought her with him when he stopped by the apartment he shared with Mathew to shower and change clothes before dinner. He'd asked Mathew to keep her company in his absence, and Mathew had been only too happy to act as Ian's stand-in.

Hell, he'd been more than half-tempted to shove Ian out of their third story bathroom window, tell Muriel the bastard bolted, and take her to dinner himself. But it was obvious by the way her eyes lit up at the mention of Ian's name that she was as into his friend as Ian was her, so Mathew stood in the back corner of the kitchen and watched his best friend walk out the door with the girl of his dreams. Then he hit the corner bar for some serious malt therapy.

Thirteen years later, she still had the same effect on him. The only difference was, rather than being Ian's date, she was his wife… his widow.

And Mathew was still a son of a bitch for coveting her.

Lucas, however, was an even bigger SOB for making Mathew an accessory in tonight's scheme.

"We need to get Muriel back in the game," Lucas said late one night the previous week when they were at the club working on their secret project.

Mathew froze, an awkward addition to the life-sized replica of the Three Graces Statue he and Lucas had just settled in place. Intuition told him what Lucas was insinuating, but there wasn't any way in hell he could be an active participant in any kind of plan that involved Muriel.

Needing to respond in some way, so he wouldn't

look like an even bigger idiot than he already did, he forced his limbs to move and stiffly walked to the crate the statue had been packed in. Shoving the broken packing material and wooden support brackets back into the shipping container, he said, "How do you propose to do that?"

"When we reveal the Roman tubs, we'll use the evening as an opportunity to draw her out of the shell she's crawled into. Who better to reintroduce her to the lifestyle than us? She's more comfortable with us than anyone. We've played with her before, and she trusts us. We need to do this for her."

No... nonononono, Mathew silently screamed while panic clawed at his chest.

Throwing the pieces into the container with far more force than he intended, he ground out a correction. "She's played with you, never with me."

Lucas huffed. "Because you never showed up at their play parties."

Damn right he'd never gone, Mathew thought again, as he ground his teeth and watched Muriel mingle with friends from his reasonably-safe distance across the room.

"Playing with Muriel" was an oxymoron as far as he was concerned, and it had been a line he'd resolved, years before, to never cross.

Where she was concerned, sex, especially when

combined with Dominance and submission, wasn't a game. She took it seriously, and if she was his submissive, so would he. He'd always known if he was ever put in the position of "playing" with Muriel, he'd be playing for keeps. And her marriage to his best friend wouldn't have mattered.

Yeah… he was that big of a bastard.

For that reason, he'd spent the past thirteen years dodging invitations to Ian and Muriel's play parties, and usually found a reason to be out of town so he didn't look like a complete ass for always declining. He'd gone out of his way to ensure he never found himself in this exact kind of hellish situation.

The first time Lucas broached the subject of easing Muriel back into the lifestyle, Mathew skirted around it. During subsequent conversations, he'd politely declined, claiming Muriel would be more comfortable with Lucas alone, especially since she'd never been with Mathew, or, as far as he knew, two men at once.

But Lucas did what he always does—twisted things around so even though Mathew knew he was being manipulated, he still capitulated and agreed to the whole massively-fucked-up plan.

Basically, Lucas asked Mathew to tie himself to the train track, then engineer the train that would leave him emotionally mutilated and scarred for life. Hell, it would be easier and less painful to turn himself over to an evil Domme for six hours of cock and ball torture.

His gaze slid to Mistress Sadie and her boy toy of the week. He winced as she grabbed his nuts and squeezed until the poor boy stood on tip-toes, gasping for breath, apologizing profusely for whatever offense had her so angry.

Okay, fuck that. Mathew wasn't into pain—giving or receiving—and in the end, he'd only be switching out one kind of pain for another. He might as well keep rolling with the emotional ass-kicking he'd grown accustomed to over the years. *That,* at least, he knew how to handle.

At least he thought he did.

He'd convinced himself he could man up and get through the evening, for the most part, unscathed. As soon as his feet hit the floor this morning, he'd begun reciting his new mantra… *Keep your distance*… and had continued repeating it throughout the day until it became an unconscious mental loop.

By the time he arrived at the club, he felt pretty good about his ability to pull off the impossible task of working with Lucas to remind Muriel of her place at the club and convince her it was safe to come back to the home-away-from home she'd loved so much. It wasn't the same without Ian around, but it was still a great place to go to be with friends.

But as he stood off to the side and watched the

members of the club welcome her back, he began to think he might've been overconfident in his abilities to see this through.

The persistent hollowness in his chest, along with his innate ability to be cold and nasty in the courtroom, had convinced him years ago he no longer had a heart. But as he watched the lights of the bar glimmer off her golden hair, he was forced to face the truth.

The painful, erratic thumping in his chest was his cold, long-forgotten heart, and he was a damned liar. There was no way he could pull this off tonight without being totally eviscerated.

And then, he truly would become nothing more than an empty shell.

FIND ALANNAH LYNNE ON THE INTERNET:
www.alannahlynne.com
www.facebook.com/AuthorAlannahLynne
twitter.com/alannahlynne
www.tsu.co/AlannahLynne